P9-EGJ-891

"We both know it would never last."

Arwenna was shaking, but determination made her continue. "I'll work for you, as I've been forced to for now, but when it's over, that's the end for us. I've never met anyone like you before, but we have no real part in each other's life."

"You seem to have forgotten something," Garth replied softly. "Neither of us has ever loved. Perhaps we aren't capable of love. Doesn't that worry you?"

"No," she said, then asked, "And you?"

"No." They looked at each other across an unbridgeable gap. The attraction was almost a tangible force. "So it might be better to work it out of our systems," he suggested. "Then we'll be free."

"You mean—have an affair?"

"What else do you think I mean?" he asked.

MARY WIBBERLEY
is also the author of these
Harlequin Romances

1968—THE WILDERNESS HUT
1994—THE WHISPERING GATE
2031—THE MOON-DANCERS
2059—THE SILVER LINK
2085—DARK VENTURER
2105—WILDCAT TAMED
2136—DAUGHTER OF THE SUN
2147—WILD GOOSE
2177—LORD OF THE ISLAND
2221—THE TAMING OF TAMSIN
2245—WITCHWOOD
2267—LOVE'S SWEET REVENGE
2277—THE DARK WARRIOR
2298—RUNAWAY MARRIAGE
2316—WITH THIS RING
2340—A DANGEROUS MAN
2364—DANGEROUS MARRIAGE
2388—MAN OF POWER

and these
Harlequin Presents

89—THE SNOW ON THE HILLS
129—THE MAN AT LA VALAISE
348—SAVAGE LOVE
390—DEBT OF DISHONOUR
419—A DREAM OF THEE
432—GOLD TO REMEMBER

Many of these titles are available at your local bookseller.

For a free catalogue listing all available Harlequin Romances
and Harlequin Presents, send your name and address to:

HARLEQUIN READER SERVICE
1440 South Priest Drive, Tempe, AZ 85281
Canadian address: Stratford, Ontario N5A 6W2

Fire and Steel

by

MARY WIBBERLEY

Harlequin Books

TORONTO • LONDON • LOS ANGELES • AMSTERDAM
SYDNEY • HAMBURG • PARIS • STOCKHOLM • ATHENS • TOKYO

Original hardcover edition published in 1980
by Mills & Boon Limited

ISBN 0-373-02418-5

Harlequin edition published July 1981

Copyright © 1980 by Mary Wibberley.
Philippine copyright 1980. Australian copyright 1980.

All rights reserved. Except for use in any review, the reproduction or utilization
of this work in whole or in part in any form by any electronic, mechanical or
other means, now known or hereafter invented, including xerography,
photocopying and recording, or in any information storage or retrieval system,
is forbidden without the permission of the publisher, Harlequin Enterprises
Limited, 225 Duncan Mill Road, Don Mills, Ontario, Canada M3B 3K9. All the
characters in this book have no existence outside the imagination of the
author and have no relation whatsoever to anyone bearing the same name
or names. They are not even distantly inspired by any individual known or
unknown to the author, and all the incidents are pure invention.

The Harlequin trademark, consisting of the words HARLEQUIN ROMANCE
and the portrayal of a Harlequin, is registered in the United States Patent
Office and in the Canada Trade Marks Office.

Printed in U.S.A.

CHAPTER ONE

'My darling sweet,' said James, looking at Arwenna with some amusement, 'the man's not all that bad.'

Arwenna gazed calmly back at him, not amused at all. 'You expect me to believe that you're having him to dinner simply out of neighbourliness? Come off it, James, since when have you been concerned about anyone who moves into the village? There's another reason you're not telling me—and until you do, my answer's no.' She stood there, tall and straight, and lifted her hand to her hip. 'I'm waiting,' she said.

For a moment his mask of amusement slipped; she saw the sulky boy underneath. But it was only for an instant, and she knew him too well to let it annoy her. 'All right,' he said. 'It's business. Dad's keen to get in well with Garth Vanner——'

'Your father is?' She lifted her eyebrows is disbelief. 'Why?'

He shrugged. 'I don't know. He doesn't tell me everything.' There was a slight trace of annoyance in his words, and she hid a grin. That was true.

'And your father wants me to come to dinner as well? He's chancing it a bit, isn't he? Doesn't he remember what Garth was like fifteen years ago when he left the village?'

'He remembers him as a tough young man who vowed he'd return one day as a millionaire——'

'And the rest? Has he forgotten? I haven't,' she cut in.

James laughed. 'You were only eight when he went. How can you remember?'

'I remember what I heard off *my* father——'

'That's all history. Okay, so your dad and his had a standing feud. So what? It was over twenty years ago——'

'And now he's come back, the new owner of Raneley Hall, and all of a sudden, because he's rich, he's made stacks of money, he's socially acceptable——'

'That's a foul thing to say!' James cut in, face pale.

Arwenna laughed. 'It's true. Twenty years ago your family wouldn't have given him or his family the time of day, and you know it. And you were only ten when he left, so you don't know the half of it either.' Her cheeks were pink. She waved her hand in a dismissive gesture. 'I'm not keen to have anything to do with him, you know that. Why me?'

'You're my fiancée,' he said, 'that's why.'

'And?'

'And Dad thought——' He hesitated.

'Yes?' she said silkily. 'Dad thought?' She paused. At last she might hear the truth.

'Well, he's supposed to have an eye for a pretty face —er—if you're here, he might be more—amenable.'

'Thanks!' She looked at him, wide-eyed with amused disbelief. 'You mean I'm a sort of decoy, is that it? A pretty face to soften him up over the hors d'oeuvres? Hah! I've had some left-handed compliments from you, James, but honestly, this takes the biscuit! And what will you do if he starts ogling me over dessert? Tell him to keep his eyes to himself?'

She turned slightly and looked into the ornate mirror over the sideboard. Her face looked back at her, a rounded, striking-looking face with long dark-lashed beautiful eyes that were usually laughing. They weren't now. She turned away and towards her fiancé.

'Please, Arwenna,' he said softly. 'Please, don't be angry. I thought you'd be pleased.'

'Pleased? I'm not. I feel as if I'm being used, if you must know.'

He closed his eyes, and Arwenna went towards him, soft-footed, graceful, and touched his arm. 'Don't you see?' she said. 'How can I be nice to him? I love you, James, you know that, but you're asking the impossible.'

'Do you?' he said bitterly. 'I sometimes wonder— you're in no hurry to get married.'

'I've told you why,' she said softly. 'Until you can break free of your father's domination.'

'He's not as bad as he was. He admires you tremendously.'

'I know. And I'm learning to get on with him, but it's an uphill battle. He doesn't actually like people who speak their minds.'

'He's accepted you,' James pointed out.

'Accepted? Yes, I suppose he has. Admires? Yes, I know that too—but only because he had no choice. Only because for the first time in his life he met someone who wasn't frightened of him.'

'You're not. You're not frightened of anyone, are you? That's what I find so—so—unusual about you, Arwenna.' James sighed. 'God, you're the most unusual, *wonderful* woman I've ever met.'

'Is that why you came chasing after me to France?' she asked mischievously.

'That's only one reason, and you know it, you little minx,' he growled, taking hold of her. 'How could you travel all over Europe, working for all those greasy foreigners?'

'I went because I wanted to,' she said, and there was a slight reminiscent smile touching her lips. 'And they weren't "greasy foreigners", they were decent families.'

'You know what I mean,' he groaned, and kissed her. 'Say you'll come tonight. Please—for me.'

She was about to open her mouth when the door to the drawing room opened and Colonel Rhodes walked in. White-haired, white-moustached, tall, erect, he was, every inch of him, the country squire, the gentleman.

Arwenna turned towards him, disengaging herself
from James' suddenly embarrassed arms. Poor James,
she thought, terrified of his father. How he ever
plucked up courage to pursue me half across France,
I'll never know.

'Hello,' she said. 'James has just been telling me
you'd like me to come for dinner tonight, to meet Garth
Vanner.'

Henry Rhodes coughed and looked at her. She knew
that she threw him completely, and she had no com-
punction about speaking her mind to him. He was so
hidebound by tradition that he found it difficult to talk
normally to anyone. Yet between them had grown a
kind of mutual respect. 'Er—yes,' he admitted. 'Lends
a bit of—er—femininity, you know. Jane is—um—
rather shy at meeting strangers, and I thought——'

'Garth Vanner is hardly a stranger,' she said, as he
hesitated. 'Considering he lived here with his family
until fifteen years ago. You did know, didn't you,
Colonel?'

'Well—um—yes, of course.' He looked uncomfortable. 'But the past is past, Arwenna. He's now a successful businessman. I think it's important to welcome
him back here, don't you?'

She smiled, meeting the Colonel's blue eyes with
her own hazelly blue, beautiful ones. 'If you say so,' she
said slowly.

James spoke for the first time since his father had
come in. 'Arwenna doesn't particularly like the man,'
he said. His father looked at him as if he had crawled
out from under a stone.

'Really?' he queried, voice cold.

'Yes, really.' Arwenna added, sensing the latent hos-
tility, never far away, between the two men, and hating
it. 'But don't worry, I'd be delighted to accept your
invitation. James persuaded me.' She smiled at the

younger man, knowing that this was important to him, knowing...

James grinned in relief, and his father unbent sufficiently to smile. 'Ah, splendid,' he said. 'Splendid.'

She didn't know why she had agreed, except that the atmosphere was so tense, the minute the older man had entered, that she had felt a strange pity for James. It was an uncomfortable feeling to have. She shouldn't feel pity for the man that she loved, only warmth, and love...

'I'll go and see Mrs Rhodes,' she said. 'If you'll excuse me?' and she smiled at them both and walked towards the door. 'What time do you want me?'

'Seven?' said James, with a look at his father, who nodded. 'I'll pick you up.'

'Seven will be fine,' Arwenna agreed. 'I'll be ready.' She went out, and heard Colonel Rhodes' voice as she closed the door. She couldn't hear the words, but the tone was hard and angry. She sighed, shook her head, and went towards the kitchen to find James' mother.

It was seven-thirty, and they were waiting for the visitor. Jane Rhodes, James' mother, a tense bundle of nerves, fluttered anxiously in from the dining room, a smudge of mascara beneath her eyes, lipstick slightly askew. 'All ready,' she said. 'Oh dear, I do hope——'

'Don't be stupid, Jane,' her husband said sharply. 'Relax.'

It seemed to Arwenna, sipping cool champagne by the window, to be a wasted admonition. There was no way Jane Rhodes would ever relax when guests were expected. Her whole life was geared to pleasing her husband, and she never fully succeeded, for how could anyone please a perfectionist? She was never able to behave as other women. Arwenna had always liked her, felt sympathy for her, and occasionally wished that she knew her well enough to tell her to tell her husband to go to hell, and walk out. She went over to her now and put her hand on the older woman's arm, sparing Colonel Rhodes, stiff and formal in black tie and evening suit, a brief glance as she did so. One more word from him ...

'I'm sure everything's perfect,' she said, smiling soothingly at Jane Rhodes. 'There's a glass of champagne I've been keeping for you,' and she led her to the leather-topped table by the window. It was light outside, cool, with a slight breeze coming in through the open windows, welcome after the heat of a July day. 'Here you are. A couple of these and nothing will matter.' She raised her glass. 'Your health.'

'And yours.' Mrs Rhodes sipped, flicking a brief glance at her husband, who stood by the fireplace. Doing his lord of the manor bit, thought Arwenna wryly, while the serfs look on admiringly.

'He said he'd be here at seven-thirty,' she whispered, so that the Colonel couldn't hear.

'It's only just——' As Arwenna said it, the door chimes went. Henry Rhodes stiffened, adjusting his tie, Jane Rhodes nearly dropped her glass, and James darted towards the door. Arwenna was the only one who made no move. I wonder what he'll look like now, she thought. I wonder. After fifteen years away from here ...

She hadn't long to wait. There were voices from the hall, and then the door opened and the man she had thought she would never see again walked in. She had heard so much about him that she felt as if she knew him. She had only a hazy recollection of him, as an eight-year-old—a vague memory of a dark, shaggy-haired youth with wildness in his blood and lightning in his fists, a young troublemaker who had hurt her parents and caused trouble wherever he went, and now she was seeing him properly for the first time, and it was such a shock that she found herself catching her breath. She didn't know what she had expected. But not this. Not this.

Garth Vanner was bigger than she had remembered. Big and dark, sleek and bold. His eyes came to hers, right across the room, and she experienced a shock that went right through her, as though the look was charged with electricity. For an instant of time it was just the two of them in the room; everything else faded away. He stood and looked at her, and she was naked, her whole being revealed to him in that moment.

Then the spell was broken, Colonel Rhodes spoke, walking forward, hand outstretched, and all was normal. The civilised preliminaries began; that primitive moment might never have been at all. 'Welcome, Mr Vanner,' said Henry Rhodes, 'nice to meet you.'

'And you, Colonel.' The men shook hands, and Henry Rhodes turned.

'My wife, Jane, my son, James—and his fiancée Arwenna.'

She was the last one with whom Garth Vanner shook hands. She stayed where she was, her glass now in her left hand, and held out her right as he walked towards her. 'How d'you do, Mr Vanner,' she said pleasantly. It had not gone unnoticed by Arwenna that the Colonel hadn't said her surname. She had no intention of telling him. Once having agreed to come, she would play her part well, be the pretty decoy for this man. For this one evening, no more. She wouldn't let any of them down, for that was not her way.

'How do you do, Miss—er——?' He raised a polite, questioning eyebrow. It was a thick, dark eyebrow, above dark grey-blue eyes that were as strong as the rest of his face.

'Call me Arwenna,' she answered, and heard the imperceptible sigh of relief from behind Garth.

'How kind. Thank you.' He turned slightly, and released Arwenna's hand. His hand clasp was cool and very firm—and totally impersonal. 'It's very nice to be here, Colonel, Mrs Rhodes.' He smiled at his hostess, and she managed a smile in return.

Henry Rhodes handed him a glass, murmuring: 'Champagne,' as he did so, and Garth Vanner raised it.

'Your good health,' he said, and drank.

Arwenna watched him, her eyes shrewdly taking in every detail of his appearance. The evening suit he wore was expensive, the shoes handmade, and if his haircut had cost him less than ten pounds, Arwenna thought, I'm a Dutchman. So this was the return of the prodigal, the local boy made good. She wondered why he had come back, after all this time. What had he done in the last fifteen years? He had made a fortune, if rumour was to be believed, and he had bought the dilapidated Raneley Hall—fact, not rumour—and Colonel Rhodes wanted something from him. And now he was here, in Grey Gables, drinking the Colonel's champagne, about to eat his food, and looking perfectly at home, as if he belonged, had always belonged, to places like this. He turned, as the conversation ebbed and flowed, and looked at Arwenna, and it was as though she had been waiting for him to do just that. His mouth twitched slightly, and he inclined his head, as if in acknowledgment of her expectations, and said quietly: 'This is a lovely house, isn't it? Do you live locally, Arwenna?'

'In the village,' she answered. 'Just a couple of miles away.'

'I see. Have you lived there long?'

'All my life,' she answered, softer, so that he had to lean his head forward slightly to catch the words.

'Really?' The bland grey-blue eyes were expressionless. 'I lived here, years ago.'

'Did you?' She put her empty glass down. 'I think dinner's ready. Mrs Rhodes is——'

He turned, nodded. 'Of course.'

They all went in, Mrs Rhodes leading their guest, the others following. Arwenna was seated opposite Garth at the beautifully laid table, the Colonel to their left at the end, Mrs Rhodes beside Garth, and James opposite his mother and beside Arwenna. Their daily housekeeper, Mrs Hedges, came with the soup, and Arwenna thought, it'll be all over the village by morning, if not tonight. The little woman's bright button eyes never left Garth's face. Arwenna wondered how much she remembered.

The dinner passed pleasantly. Whatever Mrs Hedges' faults, she was an excellent cook, and the conversation was easy, facile, due to Arwenna's efforts mainly. She had agreed to come, to help James, and once committed threw herself into the task wholeheartedly, asking Garth about Raneley Hall, the work that would be needed in it, and gradually she sensed the others relaxing, and taking their part.

There was eventually a lull, and as they waited for Mrs Hedges to bring in the dessert, Garth looked directly at Arwenna and said: 'Tell me, Arwenna, do you work nearby?'

'In Raneley itself. My aunt has a small café—but I only returned last year, when I got engaged to James. My aunt's not in very good health.'

'Ah. You'd been away?'

'Working abroad, yes.' She gave him a pleasant smile as Mrs Hedges wheeled in a trolley holding the most mouthwatering-looking confections of meringue with marron glacé purée on it, and plates of cheese and biscuits. There was silence for a few moments as they were served, the cheese and biscuits were left on the sideboard, Mrs Hedges murmured something about coffee following soon, and left them.

'This looks quite delicious,' said Garth, as they began to eat.

The Colonel beamed as though the sweet had been

all his doing, although Arwenna was willing to bet he hadn't a clue until that moment what they were going to eat. He was about to say something when Garth spoke again. 'Where abroad?'

'Italy, France, Germany, Spain, Greece,' said Arwenna.

'Good heavens!'

'I was nanny to two families over the last five years,' she explained, 'and both travelled a lot, the first in Italy and France, the second in the other three countries. It was marvellous work and I had a wonderful time.'

'I'm sure you did,' he answered. The others listened politely, as if they hadn't heard it before. The Colonel heartily disapproved of Arwenna's having worked abroad, although he had never said so directly to her, preferring to express his opinions via James. He should have been alive in Victorian times, she had often thought. He would have been extremely at home in a time when women were vigorously suppressed. It prompted her, mischievously, to say:

'I think everyone should travel when they're young, don't you? See how other people live, learn their languages, etcetera.' She gave the Colonel a warm smile. 'Don't you agree, Colonel?'

He nodded, nearly choking on his meringue. 'Indeed, yes, most interesting.'

'You learnt a language?' Garth enquired gently. 'Which one?'

As if he cared! But perhaps he had picked up someing of Colonel Rhodes' unease at her account of her travels. Garth was a shrewd man, far shrewder than anyone there, save Arwenna herself, she realised. She had seen his eyes resting on the Colonel several times during the course of the conversation, and the looks had been far-seeing.

Arwenna raised her beautiful eyes, now bright with

innocence, to him. She was going to enjoy this. 'All of them,' she answered gently, modestly.

The dark lashed grey-blue eyes met hers coolly. No surprise—merely amusement, as if he were far ahead of her in any games of words they could play. He gave a slight nod, as if of acknowledgment of her enjoyment, and she felt a small irrational flash of anger, which she hid successfully. Damn the man!

'That's most interesting,' he conceded. 'And you mastered the Greek alphabet?'

'No,' she admitted. 'But it didn't seem to matter. I mean, I was able to communicate verbally most places we went,' she shrugged delicately. It seemed to be one all, the score so far.

'Of course.' He nodded politely. 'A gift for picking up languages is to be admired indeed. It seems coincidental, but I'm looking for a translator at the moment, so I've got an interest, naturally.'

'You don't speak any languages yourself?' she queried. The others had abandoned any attempts at joining in. They all three wore polite, listening faces which didn't deceive Arwenna, nor, she suspected, Garth for a moment. As soon as decently possible, the Colonel was going to get Garth on his own, she surmised, for otherwise why would he have invited him for dinner?

'Alas, no. A smattering of French is the extent——' he gave a mock-rueful smile that managed to convey that he didn't really give a damn. Languages were for peasants. He was too busy making millions ... She wondered if she had an over-active imagination, or could really read his mind. Now she was being fanciful.

'Oh, shame. Still, never mind. I'm sure you can always find employees who're bi-lingual, can't you?'

'Indeed yes, usually.' There was a delicate pause while everyone digested the meaning of that last word, then he turned to James' mother. 'I really must congratulate you on the meal, Mrs Rhodes.'

'Thank you—Garth,' she answered. 'Some cheese and biscuits?'

'I'm not sure if I could manage——' he half stood. 'May I get them for you?'

The Colonel rose instantly. 'Stay where you are, dear fellow,' and he fetched the plates from the sideboard, giving a baleful glance towards James which was unseen by Garth.

The coffee arrived moments later, was drunk amid desultory talk regarding varieties of cheese, and personal preferences—Garth confessed a weakness for Camembert, and was persuaded to take a morsel—and then they drifted back to the drawing room, replete, whereupon the Colonel said, before Garth could sit down: 'I believe—er—Garth, that you're interested in philately?'

Garth looked faintly surprised. 'Yes, I am. I've a modest collection, but how——'

The Colonel smiled mysteriously. 'Ah, just something I read once. Got a good memory. Come into my study for a moment if you will, I've a couple of stamps you might like to see.' It was a ploy, and obvious to everyone, to get him away privately, and Garth put an interested look on his face as if he wanted nothing more than to see his host's stamp collection, gave an apologetic smile to James' mother, and went out, followed by the Colonel.

Jane Rhodes collapsed on to a settee, and Arwenna poured her a stiff brandy, whispered: 'It went off beautifully,' and sat beside her.

'Did it?' Jane Rhodes eyes were anxious and vulnerable.

'Yes, super. Didn't it, James?' Arwenna looked at him. His mother needed reassurance. She never got it from her husband.

'It seemed to. The meal was fine.' James looked levelly at Arwenna. His cheeks were slightly pink. 'You got on like a house on fire with him. Or did you?'

Arwenna's mouth twitched. Dear me, was James jealous? 'What do you mean—"or did you?"' she countered.

'There seemed to be the slightest touch of aggression flying about to me,' he responded.

Jane looked anxiously from one to the other, clearly puzzled. Arwenna wished James would shut up. 'Don't be ridiculous!' she said, laughing merrily. 'We were having a lovely chat about languages.'

'Mmm, yes—so you say.' He shrugged. 'However——'

He had picked something up after all. Arwenna was very determined not to cause Jane Rhodes any distress, and patted her arm. 'I love your dress,' she said. 'Blue suits you.'

'Thank you, my dear. And yours is lovely too. Those gorgeous flared gypsy dresses do suit you so much.' She sighed. 'Ah, what it is to be young!'

All was safely steered away. Arwenna would talk to James later, when he ran her home. Only he didn't, so she couldn't—because shortly afterwards the two men returned, looking very casual as if stamps had occupied their entire conversation, and everyone had a few drinks, and Garth concentrated all his attentions on Mrs Rhodes, until she was pink-cheeked, laughing and relaxed, and then announced, regretfully, that he would have to be leaving shortly and had had a simply splendid evening. Then he looked across the room at Arwenna and said: 'I'm going through the village, Arwenna, I'd be delighted to give you a lift home— if you need one,' and he then regarded James, who had drunk several too many glasses of port and was sitting talking to his father, next to Arwenna on one long settee. 'It would save you getting your car out again.'

James opened his mouth to speak, and Colonel Rhodes said, too quickly: 'That seems a damn good idea, eh, Arwenna?'

In an odd way, she had expected his words. In an even stranger way, she had sensed that the Colonel would reply as he had. What she didn't know then, was why. It might be interesting to find out, she thought, and lifted her eyes demurely. 'That's very kind of you,' she said. 'I am rather tired, and it's a busy day tomorrow at the café.'

Garth looked at the watch on his wrist, and stood up with a regretful smile at his hostess. Ten minutes later, farewells said, Arwenna was in his car.

CHAPTER TWO

HE drove swiftly down the long drive from Grey Gables, the door closed softly in the distance, and the three people who had stood on the steps were gone. Arwenna wondered what the atmosphere would be like; James was most definitely not pleased. She sat back in the seat, then looked at the man driving the black Lotus, hands steady on the wheel.

'Why are you going through the village?' she asked. 'Your new house is the other way.'

'You get right to the heart of things, don't you?' He stopped at the end of the drive and glanced at her. He looked as faintly amused as he had all evening, which Arwenna realised, belatedly, she had found slightly annoying.

'Yes. And so do you. So—where are you going to in the village at this time of night?'

He started up without answering, then, as they drove along the narrow country road, said: 'I'm not. It seemed a harmless enough white lie in order to give you a lift.'

'And why should you want to do that?' she asked calmly. 'James was all set to take me home. He's not pleased.'

'I could see that. I could also tell that he'd had too much to drink.'

'*That's* really none of your business,' she answered.

'True, it isn't. But I wanted to talk to you alone, and this seemed as if it might be the only opportunity.'

'Oh, I'm sure we'll meet again—some time,' she answered. But not if I see you first, she added mentally.

'Do you?' he laughed, as though he had heard those unspoken words. As if he knew that she disliked him—perhaps even why. 'I don't wait for "some time". I'm a "now" man.'

'So I've gathered,' she said dryly. 'Okay, you want to talk. Here I am, a captive audience. Fire away.'

'You're very direct.'

'You've already said that in another way. So I am, I don't believe in wasting time either—Garth.' She hesitated deliberately before saying his name. 'So what do you want to say?'

'I want you to work for me.'

She hadn't expected that. Not that. 'What?' she laughed. 'You're mad! Work for *you*? Why?'

He slowed the car down and stopped at the side of the road. The village was in sight, about a quarter of a mile ahead, street lamps shining high and yellow in the one main street. If she wanted she could get out and walk. If she wanted. She didn't—yet. She wanted to hear more about his preposterous suggestion. She was going to enjoy turning him down flat. There was no way she was ever going to work for him.

Engine off, the car silent, he turned to her. 'Mad? Tut, tut—strong word to use! You haven't heard what the job is yet.'

Arwenna too turned to face him. The interior light off, the only light was that from a high clear moon, and the car was shadowy, his face a blur.

'I don't really care what it is,' she answered. 'I don't want to work for you. I'm quite happy working for my aunt.'

'After travelling round Europe, seeing life in the big cities? You're happy here?'

'Yes. I'm also engaged to James—or had that slipped your mind?' she asked, with a touch of asperity.

'No, it hadn't. He's a fine young man—and after you'd been married to him for six months you'd be bored to death.'

Arwenna froze, shocked. She turned to open the door and he put his hand out to stop her. 'Take your hand away!' she snapped. 'I don't have to sit here and listen to your insults——'

'I'm not trying to insult you.'

'You might not be trying,' she snapped, 'but you're damned well succeeding!'

'Come off it!' he said, voice mocking. 'Do you think I'm stupid? James is scared to death of his father, his mother is equally scared—you're the only one who's not——'

'You've seen a lot of things on one visit, haven't you?' she said angrily. 'How dare you say such things!'

'I do because they're true. And you know it.' He took his hand away. 'You can't open the door anyway. There's an automatic lock. Only I can open it.'

'You've no right——'

'Maybe not. There's not much you can do about it. When we've finished our talk, I'll run you to your home, and you can get out.'

'As far as I'm concerned our talk is already finished,' she said, icy cold with anger.

'No, it's not. I've not told you about the job yet.'

'There's no point. I'm not taking it.'

'I need a secretary who's competent in several languages,' he reminded her.

'I can't type.'

'You can learn—in any case that's not the important part. The languages are——'

'Rubbish! You can employ who you like. You're loaded, aren't you? Or *supposed* to be,' she added scathingly.

'Oh yes, I'm loaded all right,' he agreed, infuriatingly calm. 'Absolutely rolling in filthy lucre—quite disgustingly so, actually.'

'God!' She turned her head away in contempt. 'You are absolutely——'

'It's what you expected me to say, so I did.' Garth put his hand to her cheek and forced her to face him. 'But I haven't finished yet.' His eyes were cold and hard, that much she could see in the dim confines of the vehicle. 'You don't like me, and I think I know why.'

'You don't,' she grated, and pushed his hand away with an abrupt, jerky movement. She didn't want to touch him; she didn't want him to touch her.

'I know your surname. It's Holmes.'

That shook her. 'How did you know?' she asked.

'I did.' He shrugged. 'I know everything I want to know—I make it my business to find out. So I know why you think I'm the loathsome creep who's come back flashing his money—the only snag is, you don't know as much as you think you do, not by a long shot, Arwenna. You were how old when I left Raneley? Five —six?'

'I was eight.'

'Then you know nothing. You were a child. You heard only what people told you.'

'And that was enough,' she said. 'Let me out here,' she added. 'I'll walk home.'

'I've not finished.'

'I have. I don't want to see you again.'

'But you're going to. If you love James you're going to work for me, and, incidentally, one day learn the truth of what actually happened years ago here.'

'Love James?' Arwenna seized on the words because they were so totally alien to the subject he had been discussing; what could James have to do with him? The evening was still warm, but Arwenna had gone cold, and pulled her black stole closer round her. It was as though everything wasn't quite real. She felt deathly cold. It was like a nightmare, a bad dream from which she had no escape. 'What do you mean? What has James got to do with——'

'Listen,' he said. 'Just listen to me. What do you think Colonel Rhodes took me off to his study for? It sure as hell wasn't to admire his stamp collection, and I'm sure you knew that as well as I did.' He tapped his finger on the wheel. 'He wants me to invest money in his clothing firm—he desperately wants that. What he didn't know is that *I* know all about his factory just the other side of Raneley. He's damned near bankrupt—but I'll bet you didn't know that, did you?'

It was a nightmare. What he was saying couldn't be true. James' father was wealthy. Not as much as Garth, obviously, but extremely well off. Everyone knew that. She shook her head. 'You're lying.'

'I'm not lying, and I can prove it. In another year he'll have to close the place, and several hundred people will be out of work. He's heavily in debt—has been for years, and now everything's catching up on him. I can save that place, and he knows it. You don't think he'd have invited me to dinner otherwise, do you? I wasn't born yesterday, Arwenna, and I haven't made my money by being taken in—I'm meeting him to-morrow, doing a tour of the place, and then we'll talk. And how those talks go depends on you.'

It was not only a nightmare, but he was mad. His

words weren't making sense. She shook her head, almost dazed with disbelief. 'How—what——' she began.

'I've told you. I want you to work for me.'

She lifted her eyes then. 'You mean if I agree to work for you, you'll agree to save his business?'

'More or less,' he agreed.

'Why? Why *me*?'

'Because, when I saw you this evening, I realised you were different from anyone I'd ever met. You've a strong, decisive personality—I need people like you on my team, and I always get what I want,' he laughed.

'You—that's blackmail,' she said with contempt.

'Yes, it is. I told him in his study that I could do with someone like you working for me. I said it quite casually, almost as an afterthought—but he got the point.'

She shivered. 'You bastard!' she whispered.

'Yes, possibly. Well, what's your answer? You do love James, don't you?'

'Of course I do,' she said. 'What are you trying to say?'

'Nothing. He must love you very much to have defied his father sufficiently to chase all over Europe trying to persuade you to come home and marry him.'

She took a deep breath. 'How did you know that?'

'I told you, I know everything I want to know.'

'You don't. There's something you don't know. And it's one reason—though there are dozens of others— why I can't work for you, despite your blackmailing efforts. I despise blackmailers, and I despise *you*,' she snapped, stiff with anger.

'Your aunt?'

'My *God*—don't say you——'

'Yes, I do. She's ill, you said. She's got gall-bladder trouble, and is working in almost constant pain, and has to be on a strict, fat-free diet—not easy when you're running a busy café. And, the hospital situation in this area being what it is, there's an eighteen month waiting list for her to have her gall-bladder removed. Unless she has it done privately, which you can't afford.'

She was silent at last. Shocked, shaken beyond words, Arwenna put her hands to her face and covered it. It was as though he were revealing her life to her, peeling away the layers of privacy until there was nothing left.

'I have a friend who runs a private clinic in London. She *needs* that operation, not constant pain-killing drugs to enable her to get through each day. She would be inside within two days, back home next week, and within a month she could be leading a near normal life —with help.'

Arwenna slowly took her hands away from her face. The palms were damp with tears. '*If* I agree, *you'll* pay for her operation?'

'Yes. And for someone to help her in the café for as long as she needs help.'

'And in return, all you want is for me to work for for you. Where? In London?'

'No. Here at Raneley Hall—and abroad.'

'Here? But the place isn't habitable yet. It'll take months.'

'Weeks. I've a team of workmen starting in two days. Next week there'll be two rooms ready at the back of the house. It's all planned. I have a lot of work to do here—I intend to do it, and to make this my base for all my future work. You can live at home—you'll just have changed your place of work, that's all.'

Arwenna sat very still, turning Garth's words over in her mind. It was all so simple and clear-cut, the way he put it. She worked for him, he would put money that was urgently needed into Colonel Rhodes' business, and he would enable her aunt to have her operation within days. There was really no choice to be made. He had successfully blocked all her escapes, literally as well as figuratively. She had the oddest feeling that if she had said no, he would just drive on, and on, and never let her out. She shivered. She wasn't normally fanciful, but she sensed that with a man as ruthless as Garth Vanner, anything was possible—and probable. He had said that she was a strong personality. She was as nothing compared to him. She had never, in all her travels, met anyone like that, and she had mixed with so many people when she had worked abroad. Wealthy people, kind, ruthless, charming, selfish—all kinds.

Never had she seen anyone remotely like Garth Vanner. He was unique, he was steel and fire, forged from humble beginnings into the person he had become. She despised him, yet at the same time she knew that he was fascinating—in a similar fashion that a snake was fascinating to a rabbit. She was no rabbit, she was a fighter, and she knew it, knew that she was capable and intelligent—and not being tried to the full, helping her aunt in the café. She loved her aunt dearly, for she had brought Arwenna up since the age of twelve, when her parents had been killed in a car crash, and she owed her much, for Aunt Daisy had the streak of independence and the adventurous spirit that had encouraged Arwenna to work abroad, 'see the world' as she had put it, at the age of eighteen.

It was one reason Arwenna had returned the previous year, when it had become increasingly obvious that her aunt wasn't well, had accepted James' fifteenth proposal of marriage, and settled back in the village life as though she had never been away. She had no regrets about returning, for her life had been rich and full on her travels, and she had many memories, and many friends, with whom she regularly corresponded. She had also worked hard, as she did now, in the café, for her aunt could do less as the time passed, and on to Arwenna the burden had fallen—a burden she shouldered willingly, and with love.

'Well?' he said, after several minutes of silence.

She looked at him, and nodded. 'I'll work for you, Garth, and I'll work hard, but only because you've made me accept. But you'll not be disappointed—because once I agree to do something, I do it to the best of my ability. You'll get your pound of flesh.' She gave a little, contemptuous smile. 'There is a time limit, though, surely? I mean, you don't expect me to work for the rest of my days for you, do you?'

'No. You are, after all, getting married soon, aren't you?'

'Don't you know? Dear me, I thought you knew everything!'

'I can hardly know something that isn't fixed up, can I?' She saw his smile in the shadowy greyness. 'Let's say eighteen months, shall we? After that you're free.' He touched her left hand, touched the ring she wore. 'Free to marry James.'

She snatched her hand away. 'I might marry him before that.'

'Really? When? You've been engaged nearly a year already. I thought the fashion nowadays was for short engagements.'

'I don't follow fashion,' she said tartly.

'You follow your heart instead. How wise! Foolish to rush into things without being sure.'

'I am sure,' she insisted.

'Of course,' he said soothingly. 'Forgive me, I should have worded it differently. It's sensible to wait until James is fully independent. He works for his father, doesn't he?'

'You know everything else, you should know that.'

'Of course I do. But he'd like to change.'

'How do you——' she began.

He smiled. 'I didn't. It was a guess. But I do now.'

Arwenna turned away. 'Drive me home, please.'

'Certainly.' He switched on, and the powerful engine roared into life. Five minutes later he had stopped outside the café door, and turned off the motor. He looked at her. 'Are you going to invite me in for a coffee?'

'No.' She turned the handle, then looked at him. 'Will you unlock this door, please?'

'Yes, when you ask me in.'

'What for?'

'I'd like to meet your aunt, tell her about my friend's clinic.'

Seething, she said: 'All right, if you must. If she's in bed, though, I don't want to wake her.'

'Of course not. However, there's a light on. Is that the sitting room or bedroom?'

She looked up through the front. 'Sitting room,' she answered.

There was a click, and the handle turned, and the door opened. Arwenna found her key and went inside, followed by Garth. She didn't switch on the light, and didn't care if he fell over one of the chairs. He didn't. He followed her closely, and up the twisty staircase at the top of which Arwenna shouted out: 'It's me, Aunt Daisy. I've got someone with me. Are you respectable?'

'As much as I'll ever be, love—come on in,' her aunt's voice floated back, and Arwenna grinned. She never moaned or complained, even when it was obvious that she was in pain. She opened the door to the sitting room and Aunt Daisy, cosily clad in warm red woollen dressing gown, feet up on a pouffe, was watching a horror film on television. Her bottle of pain-killing pills on a little table told their own story. She tried to move them, but knocked them over instead.

'Oh, Aunty, why didn't you phone?' Arwenna asked in distress, going over to pick them up.

' 'Cos it was only a twinge, that's why,' her aunt retorted with spirit, and looked over to the doorway where Garth stood watching. 'Come in, Mr Vanner, and sit down. My niece forgets her manners sometimes!' she grinned at Arwenna to show that she didn't mean it, her rosy-cheeked round face belying her health. As she had once complained to Arwenna, she had never received any sympathy as a child, because even when at death's door from 'flu, she always looked rosy-cheeked and blooming.

'And talking of phones, before I forget, James rang about ten minutes ago. Sounded surprised when I said you weren't back.'

There was a sound that might have been a small cough from Garth, and Arwenna looked round. His face was expressionless, polite. Aunt Daisy had never once mentioned his name, or the events of fifteen years before, and Arwenna was never sure if she had even heard of them. She had only moved in from London to look after Arwenna eleven years previously, and was still classed as a newcomer by older villagers.

'This is Garth Vanner, Aunt Daisy,' said Arwenna. 'Garth—my aunt, Daisy Holmes.'

He came forward, hand outstretched. 'I'm pleased to meet you, Miss Holmes.'

She looked at him, bright blue eyes searching his face. 'James said the name when he phoned,' she said. 'Do sit down, dear, it's a long way for me to look up. My, you're very tall, aren't you?'

He laughed and sat down next to her on an easy chair. 'Is that better?' he asked her.

'Much. How tall are you, then?' Arwenna left the room and went into the small kitchen next door to it. Aunt Daisy would have his sock size before she was finished! She heard his faint answer, her aunt's reply, and pushed the door closed. After putting on the kettle she picked up the telephone carefully and dialled James' number.

'Hello, James love, it's me——' she began, to be interrupted by his furious voice.

'Where the hell were you? I thought he was giving you a lift?'

'Hold it!' she cut in. 'What's with you? He did——'

'Yes. An *hour* ago——' she looked at the kitchen wall clock. It was nearly eleven. They had left at ten. Surely they hadn't been talking for nearly an *hour*?

'Well, we were talking,' she said, and at James' snort of disbelief, her temper rose swiftly. 'And he's offered me a job—and if you want to know why, why don't you ask your father?'

James suddenly became contrite. More quietly he said: 'Okay, simmer down. I'm sorry. Job? A *job*? What do you mean?'

'It's a long story,' she said wearily. 'And I'm supposed to be making coffee for him. I'll ring you in the morning.'

'Is he there *now*?'

'Yes,' she answered dryly. 'Talking to Aunt Daisy. Why? Do you want him?'

'Why did he come in?'

'To talk to her. He's going to pay for her to have her gall-bladder operation. Anything else you want to know, James, or can I go? I'm tired.'

'I don't understand——' he began, confused.

'Nor do I—look, we'll talk tomorrow.'

'Arwenna—he didn't—er—make a pass?'

'No, he didn't!' she answered. 'I wish he had, I'd have enjoyed punching him hard. But he didn't, I promise.' He's a blackmailer, she could have added, and a swine, but he didn't make a pass at me, not once.

'I'd better go, darling,' said James, 'just wanted to make sure you were home. Can I call in the morning?'

'Yes, of course. See you then. 'Bye, darling.' She replaced the receiver, saw that the kettle was boiling, and made three cups of coffee. She frowned thoughtfully. James had been understandably angry at first, then calmed down. She would tell him as much as he ought to know when she saw him. She went into the sitting room. 'Black or white, Garth?'

'White, please. No sugar.' He turned back to her Aunt.

'Have you told her?' asked Arwenna.

'No.'

'Told me what?' Aunt Daisy looked indignantly from one to the other. 'What's going on?'

'Garth has got rather a nice surprise for you,' Arwenna answered gently. 'I'll bring the coffee in. Just a moment.'

She handed them their coffees, black for Daisy, and sat down on the little stool. 'Well, go on,' she said to Garth. 'Tell her.'

He grinned at Aunt Daisy. 'You'd better put your cup down,' he said, and took it gently from her. 'How would you like to have your op within two days and be back home next week, a new woman?'

For a moment her face registered stunned disbelief, followed by shock, followed by a kind of pity. She shook her head. 'I'm sorry, Mr Vanner, I don't think that's a very funny joke,' she said. She looked at Arwenna and her eyes were sad, as if someone had let her down.

Arwenna felt her own eyes fill with tears. For this, this alone, it would all be worth it. To see Aunt Daisy's face change, as it would do in a moment, for her to *know*—it would be worth her sacrifice.

'Believe me, Miss Holmes, I wouldn't make a joke about a matter like this,' said Garth. His face was serious. 'I have a friend who runs a clinic in London— it's a private clinic, and I have his card here,' he felt in an inside pocket and handed her a small business card. 'I shall phone him in the morning, once you've given me the go-ahead, and arrange for you to go in immediately and have your operation. I can assure you that he's an excellent surgeon who treats very important people—Members of Parliament, actors, those in the public eye who need quick treatment or operations with the maximum care and minimum of waiting. And you won't have a penny to pay.'

Aunt Daisy looked absolutely dumbfounded. Her mouth opened once or twice, then she managed to speak. 'It isn't a joke, is it?'

'No, Aunty, it's not a joke,' said Arwenna, and leaned forward to clasp the other's trembling hands.

'Oh, my! But how—why——' She turned to Garth, a small smile growing bigger as she began to accept the unbelievable.

'I've blackmailed Arwenna into working for me,' he said, as if confessing something. 'She speaks several languages, and I desperately need someone to help me —and I used a little gentle persuasion, I'm ashamed to say.' He didn't look ashamed; he looked very calm and completely assured. 'I'll also arrange for help in the café, so you needn't close at all. Well, have you got used to the idea, or do you still not believe me?'

She sighed a deep sigh. 'I believe you,' she said quietly. 'And I can't even begin to thank you.'

'Then don't try.' He finished his coffee and stood up. 'If I may come over tomorrow and see you—say in the morning?'

'Yes.' Her eyes shone.

'And I will, of course, drive you down to London— I suggest you begin packing your things, Miss Holmes. They'll obviously want you in for a day before the operation for rest. I'll also have arranged, by the time I arrive tomorrow, for a couple of staff to take over the café.' He extended his hand, and Aunt Daisy took it. Her eyes shone with bright tears.

'You're so very kind,' she said. 'So very kind.'

Arwenna, watching, had to harden her heart. He wasn't kind at all, he was ruthless. Her aunt would never know that, though.

'I'll see you tomorrow,' he said, then to Arwenna: 'I'll see myself out.'

'I have to bolt the door anyway,' she said, opening the sitting room door, 'so I'll come with you.'

'Goodnight,' called Aunt Daisy as he followed her out.

'Goodnight,' he answered. 'Sleep well.'

Arwenna led him across the darkened empty café, the tables and chairs silent ghosts waiting for morning. 'You can be a real charmer when you want, can't you?' she remarked softly as she opened the outer door.

'Yes,' he agreed, 'I can. Don't forget to phone James and let him know you're home.' He smiled blandly at her from the doorway.

'I already have,' she answered.

'I thought I heard a telephone ring from somewhere when you went out to make coffee. Was he annoyed?'

'No. Why should he be? He trusts me,' she said, as bland as he.

'Foolish man!' He turned, was walking away before she could reply. 'Goodnight, Arwenna.'

She closed the door and bolted it, and then, standing back in the deeper shadows, watched him get into his car. As he started the engine and began to move, he looked right into the café, raised his hand as if in salute, and drove away. Furious—he couldn't surely have seen her, could he?—Arwenna turned away and walked straight into a table. 'Damn!' she muttered, and kicked the leg. Then she went upstairs to settle her excited aunt down for the night. She felt very tired.

Things moved fast the next morning. No sooner had James been, been soothed, and left, than Garth appeared. If Arwenna hadn't suspected that he didn't give a damn about people's feelings, she would have thought that he had remained tactfully out of sight for James' visit. His car rolled up as soon as James' had disappeared.

There were three customers in the cafe, drinking coffee with scones, three village women waiting for the bus to the nearest big town, Radford, and their weekly shopping trip. They had paid, and would leave when the bus appeared, so Arwenna took him up to her aunt who was waiting in the sitting room. It was only ten-thirty, and they would be busy in another hour until about two.

'Good morning, Miss Holmes,' he greeted her as he went in, Arwenna following. She hadn't spoken on the stairs, and given him only the briefest hello as he had entered the café. 'Are you packed?'

'Yes,' she nodded. 'You told me to.'

'That's good, because we're leaving this afternoon, after lunch.' He turned to Arwenna. 'There are two very capable women driving up from London now. They should arrive in'—he glanced at his watch—'um, an hour or so, say twelve to be on the safe side. They'll take over the running of everything for the next few weeks. You'll have an hour or more to tell them everything they need to know before you leave.'

Arwenna looked at him. Had she misheard? 'Before I leave?' she queried.

'Why, yes. You're coming to London, of course, with your aunt and me.'

'I am?' It hadn't occurred to her, but of course, how sensible it was. She would be there to help her aunt settle into a strange place. She could even stay there a couple of nights, and be at her side after the operation —if she had somewhere to sleep. She looked at her aunt, sitting so patiently and calmly there.

'I'll stop in London a day or two,' she said, 'seeing that Garth has two women coming to take over.' She went and knelt by the old woman's side. 'Would you like me to?'

'Bless you, love, it's still like a dream to me! I keep pinching myself to make sure it's real. I'd love you to stay—do you know any hotels, Mr Vanner?'

'Garth, please,' he answered. 'It's summer, a difficult time. But no problem, I know a place literally within five minutes' walk of the clinic for you, Arwenna. Hadn't you better pack as well?'

She nodded. It was all happening too fast. She must let James know, that was the most important thing. 'Yes. I'll phone James first,' she said. 'If I'd known before, I could have——'

'I've seen his father this morning, just before I came. We had one or two things to discuss, and I mentioned that you were both going to London, so he'll know later today anyway,' Garth answered. A shiver ran down Arwenna's spine. It was as though—and it was ridiculous—she was being taken over by this man.

'Nevertheless, I'll call him,' she said pleasantly.

'Then, if you'll excuse me, I have one or two things to do before we go. I'll see you in an hour. Au revoir.' He went out, leaving a small, full silence behind him. It was broken by Aunt Daisy.

'My word,' she said admiringly, 'he doesn't waste time, does he?'

Arwenna nodded. She couldn't trust herself to speak. The sensation she had, of helplessness against an overwhelming force, was totally alien to her independent spirit. But even worse was the realisation that it was only just beginning. She had met him only last night, less than twenty-four hours ago, and already her life was being organised for her. And this was only the start of it.

CHAPTER THREE

JAMES was puzzled, angry, and hurt. He too seemed to think, like Arwenna, that Garth Vanner was coolly taking over in too many areas of their lives. She hadn't told him about the blackmail over his father's firm. She hadn't told any direct lies either, but implied that her aunt's health had been the overriding factor that had persuaded her. He looked at her in disbelief. They were in the kitchen of the flat over the café, and it was nearly time to leave, and two very capable and very charming middle-aged women from an agency were already taking over downstairs, under the guidance of a still bemused Aunt Daisy.

'You said something last night about asking Dad,' he said, looking at Arwenna accusingly.

She sighed. She'd said that in temper, and she shouldn't have done. It wouldn't help James to know the truth about everything. 'Did I?' she smiled. 'It seemed as though your father wanted him to give me a lift home—or didn't you think so? Perhaps I was imagining it.' She touched his cheek. 'I'll not be away long, love. I don't mind working for him, honestly. It'll be a challenge, I suppose, using my languages, and it won't be for long.'

'How long?' he demanded.

'Let's say until I feel I've worked off the fees for the operation.' She kissed him, and he drew her into his arms and held her tightly.

'I'll get a job away from here—I'll be independent soon, I've made up my mind.'

'Have you? Good. Best thing.' Her voice was muffled, because he was holding her so closely against

him—and it was at that moment that Garth walked in.
Arwenna knew even before he spoke, because she felt
James relax his hold, then tighten it again.

'I'm so sorry.' Garth's voice was quite unmistakable.
'I'll wait in the living room.' The door closed very
firmly.

Arwenna looked up, shaking with laughter—and saw
James' furious face. 'Damn the man,' he muttered, his
eyes narrowed with temper. '*Damn* him!'

'He wasn't to know,' she said mildly. 'Anyway, it'll
do him good—let him see who belongs to whom.'

He relaxed slightly and gave a wry grin. 'I suppose
so. Just watch him though——'

'What *do* you mean? I wouldn't touch him if you paid
me. I'll be working for him, that's all. I don't like the
man. You don't need to worry.'

'Sorry.' He ruffled her hair. 'I don't like you out of
my sight. And you'll be in London with him.'

'Oh, no, I won't,' she answered. 'I'll be staying at a
hotel. I probably won't even see him, once Aunt Daisy's
settled in the clinic, don't *worry*.'

'Okay, I won't. You'll phone me?'

'Of course. Soon as I'm settled. Promise.' She kissed
him. 'See? I'll unpack my case, find a phone, and give
you my address.' It was all arranged in her mind. If
the hotel Garth knew was too expensive-looking, she
would tell him so, and find a cheaper place. In the un-
likely event of not finding anywhere, Arwenna had a
couple of numbers to ring, one the phone of two
students she'd met in Paris, and of whom she was very
fond, who shared a flat in London, the other the female
Dutch cousin of her last employer abroad, a pleasant
little woman, rather old-fashioned, who had assured
Arwenna that she had a spare room any time she was
in London. Arwenna was totally confident that either
contact would provide an answer, and had copied the
numbers and put them in her purse. But she didn't

know then of the arrangements that had already been made. She didn't know until it was too late . . .

Arwenna kissed her aunt's cheek. Daisy was sitting up in a neat bed, in an attractively furnished room which had a colour television with a remote control switch, a huge vase of exotic flowers, and a view over London's rooftops. The curtains stirred faintly in the breeze from outside, and a pretty nurse walked over and closed the window, turned and smiled at Arwenna, and said:

'Miss Holmes will be well looked after, you can be sure of that. And you may visit her any time. I'll let you say your goodbyes now, and I'll come in again when you've gone.' She beamed at them and went out, closing the door softly behind her.

'Well!' said Aunt Daisy. 'I'm here, am I? Can't believe it. Look, my own telly—I'll be able to watch Coronation Street, and all those lovely Christopher Lee films——'

'Oh, Aunt Daisy, you're a T.V. fanatic!' Arwenna laughed, and hugged her. 'You'll get spoilt here.'

'So I will—and I'll love it. Off you go, dear, Garth will be waiting for you. Come and see me tomorrow, any time now—but you go and do your shopping first, and have a look around. Do you good.'

'Window-shopping more like.' Arwenna pulled a face. 'Still, I'll go to Fortnum and Mason's and buy you a pretty jar of marmalade or something, then I can go swanking round with the bag. Goodbye, dear. Don't be watching T.V. too late.' She kissed her aunt goodbye and went towards the door. As she opened it her aunt called out:

'Thank him from me, won't you?'

'I will. Sleep well. See you tomorrow.'

The pretty nurse was waiting outside. 'Mr Vanner's downstairs talking to Mr Chisholm, Miss Holmes. He's given us the number where we can contact you if necessary.' She smiled warmly. 'And he has this number, of course.' She touched the door handle of the private room. 'I'll get your aunt settled down for a rest before dinner.'

'Not with a television in the room you won't,' said Arwenna, grinning.

The nurse laughed. 'Thanks for the warning. We'll see. We have our methods.' She produced a bottle of pills and shook them. 'One of these—she'll drift off nicely.'

'Thank you, nurse. I'll be in tomorrow. Goodbye.'

'Goodbye, Miss Holmes.'

Arwenna took the lift to the ground floor, and Garth was waiting, alone. He walked towards her. 'Ready to go?'

'Yes. But before you take me anywhere, I must make something clear,' she began, and he opened the doors and led her out as she spoke.

'We'll talk in the car,' he said. 'I need a drink.'

He had found a space nearby and as they walked towards it he said: 'Aren't you hungry?'

'Not particularly. Are you?'

'Starving!' He unlocked her passenger door and she slid in. Moments later he was weaving a way through traffic, round a corner, along a few hundred yards, and then they were going down a slope beneath a large block of flats that had a sign by it saying:

'Frensham Mansions. Car Park for Residents Only.' Garth drove into a corner by a lift, leaned over to open her door and said: 'Out you get, Arwenna.'

Obediently she did so, faintly puzzled, and he took her arm and led her to the lift. 'Where are we going?' she asked, as it rose swiftly, the small lighted discs flashing with a rapidity that left her even more puzzled.

He looked at her as he opened the door, as though his thoughts had been miles away. 'Sorry? What did you say?' he asked.

They were in a small wide corridor, thickly carpeted in a soft green. The wall lights shed a golden glow on the passage. He took some keys out and opened a door, and they were in a huge room with a picture window that stretched from one side to the other, and looked out over a rooftop view of the most exciting city in the world. Arwenna stood transfixed. The room was furnished with antiques that must have cost a fortune. Exquisite settees—three of them—covered in old gold velvet, and a deep red carpet, and two long low tables, and further away, a dining table and chairs with the rich patina of age. The velvet curtains were of matching gold to the settees.

'I said—never mind. Where *are* we?' she asked.

'My London apartment. I told you I knew a place round the corner from the clinic. This is it,' he answered, and walked down from the steps, across the carpet, towards a heavy rosewood sideboard, and opened it. 'What will you drink?' he asked.

'Something for shock,' she answered dryly.

'Ah. Cognac, yes. Do sit down.'

She went over to the window instead, and looked out, trying to place landmarks. The Post Office Tower was visible in the distance, but the rest was unfamiliar to her. She needed a map. 'We've come for a drink, right?' she said.

'Right.'

'This is a simply beautiful place. Is the hotel I'm going to stay at near here too? Only I want to talk to you about that before we leave. If it's a large expensive place, I'd rather not. I may stay quite a few days, you see, and I can guess about prices. So, if you know of anywhere—em—small——'

'You're staying here, of course,' Garth cut in, and handed her a balloon glass of mellow gold liquid. 'Cheers.'

Her eyes met his as she raised the glass to her lips.

She drank. 'No,' she said. 'Not here.'

'Don't be silly, Arwenna,' he said, in patient tones, as if addressing a small naughty child. 'It's highly practical. Literally a five-minute walk from your aunt——' he pointed out of the window. 'See that cream stone building? That's the clinic. I'm not even sure you can't see her window from here. You'll have to drape a towel on the window-ledge next time you——'

'No,' she said, not sure whether she was more amused than annoyed, but quite decided. 'I wouldn't dream of it.'

'Why not?' Hard dark eyes looked into hers.

She shrugged. 'I would think one obvious reason would occur even to you, Garth.'

'A man and a woman alone in a flat? Mmm, the conventions? You're afraid of what people might think? Or of me? Or of—yourself?'

'None of those things,' she answered promptly. Her clear, beautiful eyes, dark-lashed, looked back at him, totally unafraid. 'I'm independent—oh, I'm beholden to you already over my aunt's operation. This is a godsend, I won't deny it, but I'll pay you back eventually, never fear.'

'You will? I thought I'd made it clear——'

'You have, and I accepted, but I've had time to think about things since yesterday. I'll work hard, as I said, and——'

'But we haven't discussed your salary, have we?'

'No. Why? Are you going to pay me a pittance so that I'd never manage to be free?'

Garth laughed. 'That's a thought! You'll get good money for what you do. You've said you'll work hard, and I believe you. You'll earn your money. In fact, you can start immediately—which is one reason you're here. Some papers are highly confidential, and I wouldn't chance them being left in a hotel room.'

'You really do think of everything, don't you?' she said in reluctant admiration.

'Yes, I do.' He raised his glass. 'And I'll also tell you this. You'll see very little of me over the next few days—I'm a very busy man. This bringing your aunt down has been ideal for me, actually I'd have had to come down anyway tomorrow or the weekend. So you see,' he shrugged, 'it's worked out nicely.'

Arwenna was silent, pondering his words. So logical, eminently sensible, practical—and a mere stone's throw from the clinic. There was no argument she could put up against his.

'All right,' she said at last. 'But——'

'No buts, please. Can't you just accept things?'

She took a deep breath. 'You're taking over my life, and I don't like that.'

'Arwenna, no one can do that to you. Only if you let them.' His words were softly spoken, strangely the more powerful and decisive for that, and she realised the truth of them even as she heard them. 'I'll ring down for someone to bring up your case,' he added, 'then we'll eat.'

'Do you live here alone?'

'Yes, most of the time,' he smiled faintly. 'There are three bedrooms, and two bathrooms. Any more questions?'

'Yes. Where do we eat? Here?'

He nodded. 'I'm a fair cook, and the fridge is full. Come and see what there is, and we'll decide what we'd like.' He put down his glass on a table and walked towards the far end of the enormous room, up the steps, and opened a glass door. They were in another, wide corridor with several doors leading off. He opened one, and they were in a long, superbly fitted kitchen, with rich dark wood louvred cupboards, and tiled walls, and dark brown tiled floor. In addition to the usual fitments

there was a microwave oven. Garth opened the door of
the refrigerator and peered in as if not sure what he
would see.

'Did you stock it up?' queried Arwenna, amazed at
the variety of food within.

'No, this is a service flat. I phoned this morning
when I knew we'd be coming, and had them fill it.' He
gestured. 'What will it be? Steak, scampi, Dover sole,
chicken—name it.'

'Steak and salad?' she suggested. The compartment
at the bottom was crammed with greens.

'As good as done. I'll show you your bathroom and
you can wash while I work. How do you like your
steak? Rare, medium or burnt to a frazzle?'

'Medium, please.'

He led her to a door opposite the kitchen and opened
it to reveal a fair-sized bedroom with fitted wardrobes
in cream, a large picture window, and a large bed. The
walls were white, and had several pictures on, modern
but not unpleasing to Arwenna, who preferred tradi-
tional paintings. She looked around her. 'Very attractive,' she commented.

'Thank you. Your bathroom is there, by the window,'
he pointed to a door that she would have mistaken for
a closet door if he hadn't told her. 'It's all yours while
you're here. I have my own. I'll have your case put just
outside here.' He walked out and left her alone to look
round. The bed had a white woven coverlet that
touched the floor all round, and had a dark grey fringe
and a faintly defined flower design on it. Arwenna
went over to the window and looked out on to a
quiet grassy square with trees and benches. An old
man sat on a bench feeding pigeons, a newspaper by his
side. Beyond that more flats on three sides, as though
the garden was a private one. It was very quiet, with
no sound of traffic, or only distantly, when she listened.
She couldn't begin to imagine what the apartment cost,

but she had never in all her life seen such luxury, and she had been in some extremely costly homes on the Continent.

Shaking her head in disbelief, she opened the bathroom door and went in. When she came out refreshed after a good wash several minutes later her case stood by her bedroom door, which was ajar, and a succulent smell drifted in. Arwenna combed her unruly curly hair, smoothed on a trace of pink lipstick, and went to find her host.

A small white-topped table in the kitchen was laid for two, and he was lifting the steaks on to the plates as she went in. A bowl of mixed salad stood in the centre of the table, and a crusty French loaf cut up, and beside it a bowl of butter.

'Sit down,' he said, 'and eat. Then I'll show you your work.'

She looked at him. 'You're like the irresistible force, you know that?' she said calmly. 'I met you twenty-four hours ago—give or take a few minutes—and I'm here in London with you, and I'm not sure how it's all happened.'

He smiled slightly as he seated himself. 'And what are you? The immovable object? You know what's supposed to happen when an irresistible force meets an immovable object, don't you?'

'Trouble?' she queried dryly, and began to eat.

'Disintegration.' He helped himself to a piece of bread as Arwenna took some salad on to her plate. 'Bang! Nothing left.'

'I must remember that,' she answered calmly. Something was happening, and she wasn't sure what it was, and she certainly wasn't sure if she liked it, and it was an atmosphere in the room, a beginning of a kind of subtle tension, an awareness, a sharpness to the air. Garth Vanner was a powerful animal, sure and magnetic, and he exuded a kind of force. It was in everything he said and did, and in the way he moved. She knew why he was successful, and rich beyond a normal person's understanding, and the more time that passed, the more Arwenna realised the truth of her thoughts the previous evening, when she had known that she had never met anyone like him in her life. He gave off a kind of energy that must surely communicate itself to everyone with whom he came into contact. She shivered slightly at the knowledge, and he noticed, and asked:

'Are you cold?'

'No. You're a strange man, aren't you?'

'Am I?' He smiled.

'You know you are. You're well aware of it.'

'Are you always so outspoken with people you scarcely know, Arwenna?'

'No,' she answered promptly.

'Oh. Should I be flattered, then?' He bit into a piece of the crusty bread with strong white teeth.

'Not necessarily.' She bent to her plate and sliced a morsel of delicious steak, and ate it. He watched her, eyes unfathomable, expression serious.

'That's no answer.'

'It's all you're going to get for now. May I get myself a glass of water?'

'I'll get it.' He stood and went to the sink. 'Or would you prefer wine?'

'No, thanks. Water will be just fine.'

Garth handed her a glassful and sat down again. He was about to speak when a buzzer sounded in the kitchen. 'Damn!' He stood up, went over to a wall phone, and picked it up. 'Vanner,' he said. He looked across towards Arwenna as he listened to whoever spoke, then he said: 'All right, send her up. I'll open the door. Thanks.' He hung up and walked back to the table and sat down. 'That was the hotel porter. A friend has arrived.'

'So I imagined. A woman friend?'

'Yes.'

'Do you want me to stay in my room while she's here? If you do, will you give me some folders to look at?'

'No, you can meet her. I wouldn't dream of shutting you away.' He shook his head reprovingly. 'That wouldn't be very nice, would it?'

'I thought you were going to open the door?'

Garth finished his steak. 'First things first. Come out when you've eaten.' There came an important buzz from somewhere distant, and he laughed as he rose to his feet. 'I'll let her in before she breaks the bell.' Then he was gone. Arwenna finished her steak and carried her plates over to the sink. She would give them a few minutes and then go in. She looked down at the blue cotton dress she wore. It was one she had bought in Greece, square-necked with gorgeous embroidery at the wrists. It was her favourite dress, washed like a dream, and always made her feel good when she wore it. It was also James' favourite—which reminded her that she hadn't telephoned him. She would do so as soon as possible, or he'd be imagining all sorts of things. She went into her bedroom, combed her hair again, put on more lipstick, frowned at herself in the mirror, and went out.

Garth was standing by the window talking to a tall blonde who stood beside him. He turned at Arwenna's entrance, and, a moment later so did the woman. Arwenna found herself being stared at by the blonde, who was very attractive, dressed in a breathtakingly slim-fitting dress in some swirly flame-coloured material. The look was a rather puzzled one, but it vanished a moment later as Garth said: 'Arwenna, meet Lucy Moore. Lucy—Arwenna Holmes.'

'Hello, Arwenna,' said Lucy, in a voice that matched her face. Very attractive, slightly husky.

'Hello.' Arwenna walked slowly down the steps, and

towards them. Lucy half turned towards Garth again
—not in a rude manner, but as though continuing a
conversation.

'So Rollo persuaded me, as I was passing, to call in.
He'd been trying to get you all day, darling.'

'We only arrived here half an hour ago. Sorry, Lucy,
but I think I'll give this one a miss. I've got a heavy
day tomorrow.'

'He said he asked you weeks ago and you said yes.'

'Did he? So he did. I simply forgot. In fact if it
hadn't been for bringing Arwenna's aunt here to Bob's
clinic, I dare say I'd still have been in Raneley.'

She made a small moue of exasperation. 'Really,
Garth! You know Rollo wants you to meet his Dutch
chum——'

'Damn! So he does. Look, Lucy, let me get you a
drink, and I'll call him now. I dare say I can squeeze a
meeting in tomorrow. Sit down and talk to each other.
What'll it be?'

'Got any champers?' asked Lucy, with a winning
smile in the vague direction of Arwenna, and seated
herself nearest the window. 'I had a heavy night last
night—you *know* how it is. Couldn't touch anything
stronger.' She passed a delicate hand across her forehead.

'There's a bottle in the fridge. Be back in a moment.'
Garth strode away, leaving Lucy and Arwenna alone.

'Are you an old friend of Garth's?' asked Lucy, with
an innocent look at Arwenna—taking in the engage-
ment ring in passing.

'No,' conceded Arwenna, wondering what Lucy
would say if she told her the truth, 'I've not known him
long. But he drove my aunt down to his friend's clinic
today, and we came back here for a meal.'

'Oh, shame. Nothing serious, I hope?' Lucy spoke
politely, but distantly, as if her mind was on other
matters.

'Gall-bladder.'

'Dear me! Has he known your aunt long?'

Garth returned as Arwenna answered that no, he hadn't really, and he opened the bottle and poured out three glasses. 'I'll phone Rollo,' he said. 'Take your time. Help yourself to more.' He went to a telephone by the window, picked up the receiver, and dialled.

'Rollo gives *the* most *fabulous* parties,' said Lucy, as Garth began to speak. She kept her voice low, and Arwenna, sitting beside her, had to lean forward to catch the words. 'He'll be *furious*!'

'You're going, I take it?' asked Arwenna.

'Wouldn't miss it!' was Lucy's cheerful answer. Her eyes were a bright blue, heavily made up, and Arwenna suddenly felt as if the other's face was familiar.

'Have I seen you somewhere before?' she asked.

Lucy smiled. 'I dare say. I've been in several adverts on T.V. Nothing spectacular, but——' she gave a modest shrug.

'Good gracious! You're the girl in the Verini Vermouth ads!'

'The same. How clever of you!'

'How fascinating,' said Arwenna. 'I've never met anyone from television before. My aunt will be green with envy!'

Lucy laughed. Arwenna sensed a slight thaw in her manner, though it had been pleasant enough all along. 'It's a job like any other,' she said casually, 'but still, it's nice to be recognised, I must admit. And what do you do, Arwenna?'

'From today, I'm working for Garth. I speak several languages, and he needs a translator.'

'He does?' Lucy's beautiful face registered blank surprise. 'But he——'

'All settled,' said Garth, as he put the telephone back and walked over. 'We're all going, but I'm not staying late. You don't mind, do you, Arwenna?'

Lucy's face was a sight to see. Several things appeared to be in her mind, and uppermost was—could it be anxiety?—Arwenna wasn't sure.

'Of course not,' Arwenna answered. Why not? Lucy, despite her slight agitation, was pleasant enough, and Arwenna enjoyed meeting people, and it was certainly a better alternative to spending the evening alone with Garth.

'That's settled, then.' He looked at his watch, poured out more champagne for them all, and added: 'We'll all go together from here. Where's your car, Lucy?'

'Outside.'

'Give me the keys, and I'll get Fred to put it in the car park. You won't want to drive home after you've been drinking, will you?'

'No, but I was going to go home and then get a taxi.'

'Save time. He says to go now, before it gets too crowded.'

'But I must change——' began Lucy.

'Rubbish! You look gorgeous as you are, and you know it. Besides, if I know Rollo's little do's half the guests will be wearing jeans and tee-shirts!'

Lucy gave Arwenna a helpless look. 'There's no point in arguing with him, as you'll find out if you're going to work for him, darling.'

Arwenna gave a noncommittal smile, and Garth went on: 'I'll have a shave, change my shirt, and we're off.' He finished his glass, and Arwenna stood up.

'May I phone James before we go?'

'Sure. There's one in your bedroom.' He walked out. Arwenna turned to Lucy, about to excuse herself, and saw a look of stunned disbelief on the other's face. Lucy's eyes were wide.

'Are you *staying* here?' she asked.

'Yes.' Arwenna sat down slowly. 'Why?'

Lucy shook her head. 'Oh!' was all she said. Arwenna

felt an irrational flare of annoyance, but hid it. It wasn't, after all, *her* fault that she was staying.

'Why?' she demanded, and Lucy looked at her, perhaps sensing Arwenna's impatience.

'Has he mentioned Marcia?' she said.

'No. Who's she?'

Lucy gave a faint smile. 'An—acquaintance of mine, and a very good friend of Garth's.'

'A—*very* good friend?' queried Arwenna with delicacy.

Lucy nodded. 'Mmm. And she'll be there tonight.'

'Which is why you looked rather anxious when you knew *I'd* been asked to the party.'

Lucy's mouth twitched. 'Did I? You're very quick, aren't you?'

'Yes. So are you.'

They looked at each other, and there was a sudden mutual understanding. 'You'd better tell me,' said Arwenna, 'before Garth gets back. Is Marcia the jealous type?'

'You could say that.'

'And she's a friend of yours?'

Lucy laughed. 'We're both models. We both do T.V. work. I've known Marcia for a couple of years.'

'Doesn't she mind you coming here alone?'

'Not a bit. Garth and I like each other, but we don't fancy each other, and she knows it. I've got a special boy-friend, so as far as Marcia's concerned, I'm no threat. But, oh *dear*, she won't like you.'

'Lucy, I'm engaged, and I love my fiancé. I have no interest in Garth at all, I promise you,' Arwenna assured her.

'I believe you, ducky. But—as they say—try telling that to Marcia.'

'Is he in love with her?'

Lucy frowned. 'I don't think so. She'd like him to be,

but he's an elusive bird, is our Garth. She's good company, fantastically witty, beautiful—got loads of men after her, but only wants one.'

'Well, the party should be interesting,' said Arwenna, 'if nothing else.' She stood up again, and Lucy said quickly, quietly:

'Arwenna, a word of advice——'

Arwenna paused, half turned away. 'Yes?'

Lucy pulled a face. 'Be careful.'

'You mean—keep out of her way?'

'Something like that.'

'Thanks for the warning. But why?'

'Why what?'

'Why tell me? She's your friend—I'm nobody really. I shouldn't even be there.'

'She can try and make you feel small—she would spoil your evening. It's just a friendly warning, no more,' Lucy explained.

Arwenna nodded. 'Then thank you, Lucy. I'll remember your advice.' She gave her a reassuring smile. 'If you'll excuse me, I'll go and phone my fiancé.'

Lucy watched her go, then she bit her lip and shook her head. Arwenna wondered fleetingly, as she went into her bedroom, if Garth had made sure she was invited, knowing what Marcia's probable reaction would be. It seemed likely. Perhaps he enjoyed playing people off against each other. If so he would be disappointed. They seemed, from what she had just heard of Marcia, an ideally matched pair, well suited in every way. Even Lucy's suggestion, that Marcia would be jealous, was preposterous. She began to laugh softly at the thought as she picked up the telephone receiver from the bedside table, and started to dial.

Three hours later, she wasn't laughing.

CHAPTER FOUR

THE room in which the party was being held was so crammed with people that it was a simple matter to avoid anyone. Arwenna had been introduced to so many that she had forgotten half the names instantly, had been chatted up by four good-looking men—not all at once—and plied with drink until she was pleasantly muzzy; and was thoroughly enjoying herself. She had seen little of Garth since arriving, had managed a brief conversation with Lucy, and their host, Rollo, a slim middle-aged man with silvery over-long hair and delicate manner who went around kissing everyone indiscriminately, and was extremely tipsy, and she had seen Marcia twice, in passing. She was stunning-looking, and always at the centre of a crowd of admirers, and Arwenna began to think that Lucy had over-dramatised everything—even though with good intentions—until she went to the bathroom which led off a main bedroom and when she came out Marcia was waiting for her.

She noticed two things straightaway. The bedroom door was closed, and Marcia was icily, coldly, angry. It was such a contrast to the laughing, beautiful face that Arwenna had glimpsed before that it was almost as though this were a different woman. 'Are you Arwenna?' Marcia asked.

'Yes, I am,' Arwenna smiled, only slightly puzzled. She had, after all, been warned. 'And you're Marcia.'

'And I want a private word in your ear, dear,' said Marcia silkily.

'Fire away. We're alone—but not for long, I should imagine,' Arwenna answered cheerfully.

'What I have to say won't take long. What's your little game with Garth?'

'Game?' Arwenna laughed. 'What do you mean? I'm working for him—hasn't he told you?'

'Yes, he has. But he doesn't normally have his employees living at his apartment.' Marcia's eyes glittered coldly.

'Oh, I wouldn't know about that. I only met him yesterday,' said Arwenna, hearing the other's indrawn hiss of breath with some satisfaction.

'You little *tramp*!' spat the other. 'There's only one woman stays there—and that's me. I don't know what the hell you're thinking of, but *you* can leave tonight, do you hear? *I'll* be going back there with him after the party and we won't want you.'

'Where do you suggest I go?'

'I don't give a damn, quite frankly. Just go.'

'And what would I tell him?'

Marcia moved nearer to her. She was as tall as Arwenna, dressed in a shiny cat-suit in pink, and very high heels. She should have looked ridiculous, but she was very elegant. 'That you can't stay—what else?'

'Suppose I tell him you've threatened me?' asked Arwenna.

'He wouldn't believe you—and I'd deny it.' Marcia smiled slowly, cat-like. 'He'd want to believe me, anyway—if you see what I mean.'

'Oh, I see all right. You're his mistress?'

'And don't intend to be usurped by some country yokel. You get my meaning?'

'I think so.' Arwenna widened her eyes innocently. 'And I suggest you tell him so yourself, because I have no intention of leaving until I'm ready. You get *my* meaning?'

Marcia reached out and slapped Arwenna's face hard. It hurt. Arwenna caught her breath in shock, and the other said, low and shaking, 'You'll regret it—I mean it! He won't always be there——'

Slap! Arwenna stepped forward, lashed out with all her strength, and caught Marcia a stinging blow across the cheek. She moved even faster then, reached out and grabbed Marcia by the shoulder and shook her hard.

'Don't you ever dare hit me again,' she said furiously. 'And don't threaten me. I'm not in the least bit interested in your lover—as far as I'm concerned, you're welcome to him!'

Marcia wrenched herself free, gave a cry, and launched herself on Arwenna. Without even thinking about it, Arwenna twisted round, bent, caught the other's arm, and sent her sprawling. Before Marcia could get her breath, Arwenna was standing over her, and said: 'I warned you—*dear*—I'm a damned sight stronger than you, and I'll finish what I have to say, and you'll damned well listen, you vicious bitch. I'm going to tell him what you've done, and if he wants me to leave, I will—but only if *he* wants me to. Not *you*. Do I make myself clear?'

Hate-filled eyes glared back at her. Arwenna pulled Marcia to her feet as a pounding came on the door, and a voice: 'Hey, what's going on?'

She opened the door, which Marcia had bolted, and Lucy stood there, eyes horrified. 'Hi, Lucy,' said Arwenna. 'Marcia's in there,' and she walked out and back to the party. The first person she saw, waiting at the end of the corridor, was Garth.

'What's the matter?' he demanded, face hard.

'Don't you know?' Arwenna asked. She suddenly realized that she was shaking, and rubbed her bare arms. 'I've just been threatened by your mistress, who seemed to think I was after you.' He glanced along towards the closed bedroom door. A raised voice could be heard from behind it.

'You're joking,' he said.

'Don't be stupid,' she snapped. 'If I was going to make something up, it wouldn't be that. She slapped my face, if you must know.'

He started to walk towards the door, and Arwenna caught up with him and held his arm. 'Just a moment,' she said. 'You'd better hear the rest of it. I hit her back harder—and if she tries anything with me again, I promise you she'll be sorry. You can tell her that. I'll wait here. If you want me to leave your flat you'd better find me a hotel.'

Garth looked down at her. 'There's no question of that,' and he pushed open the door and went in. Arwenna heard Marcia's loud sobbing, and the next moment Lucy came out. The door closed, and Lucy looked at Arwenna.

'My God!' she whispered. 'What happened?' Her face was white with shock.

Awenna shrugged. 'You were right. I apologise—I thought you were exaggerating. She told me she wanted a word with me, and then told me to leave Garth's flat —I refused, so she hit me—I hit her back—and she came off slightly worse in the fight that followed.'

'Stay there, and I'll get you a drink,' said Lucy. 'There's a loo at the end of the corridor. If anyone else comes along, direct them there. There's a big scene going on in the bedroom.' She pulled a face. 'Won't be a moment.'

She came back a minute or so later holding a glass. 'Brandy,' she said. 'Drink that. I'm sorry, Arwenna, I saw her go after you, but I waited a while—I should have knocked sooner. She'd locked the door, you see.'

'Yes.' Arwenna shivered. 'I'm sorry. I don't like un-pleasantness, but she got me so mad——'

'She's had it coming to her for a while.' Lucy shook her head. 'She's always had her own way, always—I suppose she imagined you'd meekly take everything from her, as most people do.' She looked at Arwenna with sympathy-filled eyes. 'I did try. She's always been so careful not to let Garth see her temper, but now——' she shrugged.

'I hope she won't take it out on you,' said Arwenna.

Lucy grinned slightly. 'She'll be sorry if she tries! I'm not a shy little creature myself, believe it or not.'

'I'm sure you're not.' The door opened, and Garth came out. He looked at Lucy

'Lucy, do you want to stay, or would you like a lift home? I think it's time we left.'

Lucy grimaced. 'Hadn't I better go and pick up the pieces?'

He shook his head. 'Marcia has a—headache. She'll come out when she's ready. But it's up to you.'

Lucy nodded. 'Give me a minute.' She left them alone. The noise of the music was loud, the voices nearly as much so.

Garth looked at Arwenna, and a muscle moved in his jaw. 'I'm sorry about this,' he said.

'Don't apologise. You could have warned me it might be hazardous working for you, though. I'd have been more prepared.'

'It won't be in future,' he assured her.

'I hope not. I'm not used to being physically assaulted.'

'But you gave better than you got.'

Arwenna smiled slightly. 'I've worked in Italy and Greece and I've learned how to look after myself.' Sudden, raw tension sparked between them, and she saw his face change, was aware that her own had too. She felt lightheaded, almost dizzy. Nothing had prepared her for this.

'I was right about you,' said Garth, as if choosing his words carefully. 'You are unique.'

'What did you say to her?' she asked breathlessly. She wanted to move away, but couldn't. She wanted to escape, but there would be none.

'Not a lot. I told her we were through, then I came
out.'

She shivered. That was it, with him. Finish, the end.
She was glad she didn't love him; to do so would be to
become vulnerable. 'You are hard,' she whispered.

'Yes, I am.' He took her arm as Lucy came out, alone.
'Let's go.'

They were driving away before Lucy spoke. 'Marcia
was crying,' she said. 'I didn't like leaving her.'

'Marcia will recover. She's going away to Malta on
a job in a couple of days, and you can bet she'll be all
right for that.'

'I didn't think you could be so hard, Garth.'

'I didn't realise that Marcia had such a temper until
now. I'd never believed the things I'd heard, and I
thought it was jealousy because she's so successful, but
now I realise it wasn't.' He turned and grinned at Lucy
as they drew to a halt outside a block of flats. 'Thanks
for breaking it up, Lucy. What time do you need your
car for tomorrow and I'll see you get it?'

'I'll collect it in the morning.' She slid across the
back seat to the pavement side. 'Thanks for the lift.
Goodnight, Garth, Arwenna.'

'Goodnight.' He waited until she had gone inside the
main entrance and drove on. Fifteen minutes later they
were entering his apartment.

Arwenna awoke from a deep sleep to see the sun
streaming in through the open curtains. Someone was
knocking at her door.

'Come in,' she said, and Garth came in with a cup
and saucer.

'Good morning. I've brought you coffee. I'm going
out in a few minutes.' He put the cup down on her
table, and beside it, a key. 'I don't know when I'll be
back. There's a key for you to let yourself in. Tell the
hall porter your name and he'll let you up in the lift. If

you want to go shopping, get a taxi—he'll call one for you. It goes on my account. If you want to phone anyone, feel free. I'll phone if I'm any later than you. Oh, and there's toast ready in the kitchen. Want some?'

There was no tension now. He was being polite, the perfect host, in fact. 'I'm rather hungry,' Arwenna confessed. 'I'll get my robe on and come out.'

'Okay, I'll take this coffee back and have one with you before I go.' He took the cup and went out, closing the door after him. Arwenna picked up the key, looked at it, and put it down. Then she got out of bed and padded barefoot to the bathroom.

In the kitchen Garth had set out her toast with butter and marmalade, and two cups of coffee. He was dressed in a very conservative charcoal grey suit and tie, and a white shirt.

'Sit down and eat,' he said.

Arwenna obediently sat down and began to butter toast. 'Want some?'

'No, thanks, I've eaten. Are you all right? Did you sleep well?'

'Yes, thanks—and yes, like a log. I always do.'

He gave a faint smile. 'Good. Will you see your aunt today?'

'This morning, if I can.' She had no intention of taking a taxi anywhere.

'Give her my regards when you do.'

'I will.'

Garth finished his coffee and stood up. 'I'll see you later. Goodbye.'

'Goodbye.' She waited, and heard the outer door close. She was completely alone. It was a strange feeling, to be in his apartment alone. She hadn't even seen all round it; there had been no time after her arrival. It seemed to Arwenna that he must trust her to leave her there when he scarcely knew her.

That was an odd feeling to have. She finished the

toast and went to shower and dress. Afterwards she walked round the huge main room, just admiring, not touching anything. The view drew her to the window and she looked out to see rooftops gilded in the sunlight, and tall buildings, and people and cars far below. All was so silent, as if she watched a film, and she saw that the window was double-glazed. A flash of movement caught her eye, and a pigeon flew past, shadowing the sun for an instant of time. Arwenna looked round again, and wondered why Garth should want to return to Raneley when he had this. She had met many of his friends the previous night, before her regrettable encounter with Marcia, and they were a world away from the people of Raneley, like a different race. She hugged her arms to her sides. He was one of them, no longer the village boy. He was worldly, hard, quick-thinking. Why then return? The slower pace of village life would not be for him, surely?

She might as well go out. The key was safely in her handbag, and she had sufficient money for small purchases, as well as her banker's card, which she didn't intend to use at all, but it was nice to have, in case ... She grinned to herself. Time to go.

Ten minutes later she was walking into the clinic, and two hours after that was gazing round Fortnum and Mason's in wide-eyed wonder.

She returned to the apartment at three, with a small stack of books from a secondhand shop, and a jar of strawberry jam from Fortnum's. Her legs ached from walking, and she had been lost more than once, and had to ask until she had bought a map. She put them down in her bedroom and went to make herself a cup of coffee in the kitchen.

Now what? Did she wait for Garth to return, like an obedient employee—or slave—or did she go out again? She sighed, took her coffee into the large room, sat by the window, and drank it slowly while she thought about it.

The shrill ring of the telephone startled her, so loud was it in the silence. She picked it up and gave the number.

'Hello, Arwenna, it's Garth. I've tried several times to get you.'

'I've only just got in,' she answered.

'So I guessed. Look, I'm tied up in a meeting for an hour or so. Do you want to do some work for me?'

'Yes.'

'My study's two doors along from the kitchen. Go in, and on the desk you'll find several folders relating to property abroad. Read them, but don't bother to write anything down yet, just translate mentally. See how you go. If you see anything you feel I ought to know, jot down notes—you'll know what I mean. There are several foreign dictionaries on the study bookshelves. You can practise typing as well. Paper in a drawer——'

'I don't like going through drawers if you're out,' she protested.

'Anything that's open isn't private. Feel free. If you need me, call me at this number—got a pencil?' Arwenna opened the small notepad at the side of the telephone. There was a pencil attached to it.

'Yes.' She wrote the number he gave her and closed the book.

'Only phone if it's important. If the phone in the study goes, you needn't touch it. It's on the answering machine, and is a separate line. Any questions?'

'No.'

'Right. Goodbye.' The line went dead. No, you certainly don't waste time—or words, Arwenna thought, and pulled a little face. At least her problem was solved.

Feeling not a little curiosity, she pushed open the door next but one to the kitchen, and went into a large room. It was full of bookshelves, filing cabinets, a huge desk with an electric typewriter in the centre, several folders neatly beside it, and a desk calendar.

The walls that weren't lined with books were poster-filled, pictures of large villas and houses and castles. There was also a large wall calendar, with the whole year spread out at a glance. She looked round her, taking it all in. A telephone was on a table by the window, attached to a machine. Arwenna went over to the desk, sat down, picked up the top folder, which was labelled, 'France', and opened it. She was confronted with a thick wedge of papers, illustrated brochures of property in France, of all types, and all in French. She put it aside and opened the next folder, marked, 'Italy'. The same type of papers, but now, not surprisingly, in Italian. There was a week's work here alone.

Arwenna opened a few desk drawers, found a note-pad and ballpoint pen, carried the two folders with them back into the main room, settled herself down by the window after first making a cup of coffee, and began to read. She started on the French papers, found that the mental effort of translating as she went along tiring at first, then, as her mind adjusted, becoming easier until she was skimming quite rapidly over each separate brochure.

She laid each one neatly face down when finished, on the table, and that pile grew, and the unread one got smaller, and a pattern was beginning to emerge, which she found intriguing. She picked up the pad and started making notes.

Time passed, but she was scarcely aware of it, until she heard the door open and footsteps. She looked up to see Garth coming in, then at her watch.

It was past seven o'clock. He flung his briefcase down and walked over to her. 'Busy?' he queried.

She stretched. 'Yes. I'd lost count of time. I must have been sitting here nearly four hours!'

'There's dedication.' He seemed amused about some-thing. 'Anyone ring?'

'Not in here. The phone in your study went several times, but I left it.' She blinked. 'I'm hungry—I've just realised.'

'Did you have any lunch?'

'A couple of sandwiches in a snack bar while I was shopping.'

'We'll eat out. Go and do your hair, or whatever it is you women do.'

'No, I'll stay here, thanks all the same.' She picked up a brochure in danger of sliding to the carpet. 'I've nearly finished the French folder.'

'Well? Anything strike you?'

'Yes. I've made notes. Want to hear them?'

Garth sat down. 'Fire away.'

She looked at him. 'Is there something you find funny? Have I a smut on my nose or something?'

He peered closely at her face, and Arwenna felt vaguely annoyed. 'No, all's clear. I don't find anything funny—I was just surprised at your dedication. Have you been through all these?' He tapped the larger stack.

'Yes. It's what you asked me to do.'

He shook his head. 'You're a quick reader.'

'I know. Once I'd started it all came back. The first couple were a strain, then it was just like reading Eng-lish.'

'Amazing! I chose right, picking you to work for me. You're going to be very valuable. How do you feel about going to France in a week or so when your aunt's recovered from her operation?' He said it as casually as if he'd asked her if she would like a drink.

Arwenna dropped the papers on the table. 'What?'

'France—next week—once Aunty's home?' he re-peated in abbreviated form, face expressionless.

She shook her head. 'But—Raneley Hall—James' father——' then belatedly : 'James——'

Garth held up three fingers and pointed to the first. 'There's a team working from tomorrow at the Hall, under the supervision of a very competent foreman. Two—I'll see James' father immediately we return to Raneley next week. It's Wednesday today, your aunt has her op tomorrow morning, and all going well, should be out by a week on Friday. We'll fly to Paris a week on Monday, by which time all will have been arranged with the Colonel. Three—James. Well, what about James? He knows you're working for me, doesn't he?'

'Yes, but not going abroad with you.'

'You object?'

'He might—he will——' she began.

'That wasn't my question. I said, do *you*?'

It was there again, the indefinable blurring of the senses in his presence that made Arwenna feel as if she was being swept along with a tide, helpless, unable to resist anything. 'You don't understand,' she said feebly.

'It's quite simple to me—it seems it's you that doesn't understand,' he answered.

'No. You said—when you *blackmailed* me into this job,' she added, emphasing that important word, 'that you'd be working from Raneley. You never said anything about going abroad with you.'

'True, I didn't. But flexibility is the key word for my staff. My plans are changing all the time. It's now rather essential that I go, and I want you with me. I've got some important deals lined up that will mean a lot of money. I don't have to remind you that your aunt is in the clinic, and the operation goes ahead tomorrow —so it's a bit late for you to back down out of our arrangement now.'

Arwenna jumped to her feet. 'That's——'

'Blackmail? Can't you find another word for a change?'

'No, damn you, I can't!' she blazed, suddenly angry, and he stood up and grabbed her arms.

'Calm down! You'd think I was going to torture you —I'm offering you a chance to go to France, travel round with me visiting beautiful places—a chance which, I might add, any one of a number of my staff would give their eye teeth for—and you're throwing a tantrum fit to——'

'I'm not!' she stormed, and pulled herself free. 'Anyone who doesn't agree with *you* is childish. Hah! That's typical male logic. I don't buy it, so don't try it again. You've led me into this gradually and cleverly, haven't you? One little step at a time and she won't notice. Well, I'm not as stupid as you think, Mr Vanner —I'm supposed to be terribly flattered and honoured. I'm not—I'm engaged to James, and I'm going to marry him, and *that's* all I want. Your money and your power doesn't impress me *one bit*—so why don't you take one of your starry-eyed secretaries or whatever, and do them, and me, a favour?'

'For one very obvious reason,' he said, apparently unmoved by her tirade. He looked her slowly up and down. 'Because you've got more personality in your little finger than most of them have in their whole bodies. Because you're different—and because you're bloody well wasted working in a café and I suspect you know it.'

'That's a horrible thing to say!' she burst out. 'Aunt Daisy——'

'Aunt Daisy is a lovely gentle person whom I respect and admire, and she's happy and content to run her café, and that's as it should be. But you've no place there, and you know it. The world can be yours, and all that's in it—yet you go and get yourself engaged to a young fool like James——'

He got no further, Arwenna stepped forward, incensed, and struck out at his face. But her hand never connected. He gripped her wrist, swifter than thought, and held it away from him.

'You don't like the truth,' he said harshly. 'But don't go and hit me because I tell you the things you deny. We are two of a kind——'

'Never!' she spat, eyes narrowed.

'Two of a kind,' he repeated relentlessly, still holding her as though she had never interrupted. 'Fighters, both knowing what we want out of life, although you've missed your way lately.'

'You're talking rubbish,' she cut in. 'And let me *go*!'

'When I choose to,' he answered. 'When I've finished what I'm going to say.'

'You've finished already as far as I'm concerned,' she snapped, and tried to pull her hand free of his. 'I'm *not* like *you*. You're ruthless, hard——'

'Perhaps. Not in that sense. You're neither of those things—but you have other qualities that we both recognise in each other, whether you choose to admit them or not. I saw them in you straight away, as soon as I met you—which was when I knew that I wanted you.' His eyes were dark and serious, strangely so, as he looked at her, and the last six words that he had said seemed to stay there, echoing and re-echoing in Arwenna's mind, double-edged, and meaning more, much more than what had gone before. She was still, no longer trying to free herself from his grasp, and it was as if in a strange way she knew that everything had been leading up to this moment. As if something had been said which would never be taken back.

She could feel Garth's hand clasp on her wrist, feel every inch of his skin on hers, and his hand was warm and strong, and the touch was an electric current that coursed through her very blood and made her temples pound and the pulse beat rapidly at her throat. Every-

thing about him became etched sharply in her awareness. It was as if she saw him with all her senses, as if
she could touch him, hear him, with her eyes. The tall
powerful size of him, the smooth tanned face, not quite
as hard now. The eyes, a clear grey-blue, dark-lashed,
his mouth wide, sensual, full-lipped, nose straight, big,
not too big, dark hair that was smooth and healthy-
looking, a thick powerful neck on equally powerful
shoulders. All this she saw as if seeing him for the first
time, and she couldn't look away, couldn't move.

'I—don't—want—you,' she managed to say, and it
was as if she had to force each word out separately.

'But you will,' he said softly, insistently.

'No!' The word was jerked from her.

He smiled, then he released her hand, and she
rubbed it as if to erase his touch. 'We'll have a drink,'
he said. 'Then we'll go and have a meal.'

'I don't want to go out with you,' she answered. 'I
don't want to go anywhere with you——'

He walked away from her, poured two glasses of
brandy and brought them back. 'You've just had a
shock,' he said. 'Drink that, and you'll feel better,
Arwenna. We'll talk about France and the folder, over
our meal.'

'Don't you ever listen to me?' She swallowed some
brandy and gasped as it went down, warm, soothing—
and made her feel a little better.

He looked at his glass, held it up to the light, sipped
a drop. 'Cheers,' he said. 'What did you say?'

'Damn you! You *don't* listen. 'I'm staying here. I'll
cook something for myself——'

Garth sighed. It was quite a patient sigh as though
he was prepared to humour her. 'I've a table booked for
eight o'clock at a delightful Italian restaurant not ten
minutes from here. We'll walk if you like. I've had a
hellishly busy day and need a break. I do not want to
eat in. Do you understand? We'll have a pleasant meal

and return here, then I will go into my study and work
for a couple of hours, then go to bed. I've been working hard so as to keep my morning free tomorrow so
that I can wait with you for news from the clinic. Now,
am I asking too much?'

Arwenna's resistance had been gradually crumbling
away as he spoke, and his last words clinched it. Why
hadn't he said that before?

She nodded. 'You—you've done it again, haven't
you?'

'I always do.' He finished his brandy. 'I'll go and
change. We'll leave in twenty minutes. Can you be
ready for then?'

'Yes.' She put her glass down. Then, because it had
to be asked, and while there would never be a right
time, because she didn't really want to hear the answer,
the sooner she asked it the better, she said: 'Before
you go—what did you mean when you said, "I knew
that I wanted you"?'

'I thought you'd never ask. Don't you know?'

'I want you to tell me,' she answered very quietly.
Her mouth had gone dry.

'How does any man want a woman? I want to make
love to you—to be with you, to know you in the fullest
sense of the word——'

'And is that why you brought me here?' she gasped,
shocked, even though it was the answer she had sensed
she would hear.

'No. What do you take me for? That would be crude
in the extreme, to put you in the difficult position of
having nowhere to stay.'

'Then France? Is that what you expect?'

He smiled slightly. 'I'm not a fool, Arwenna. Nor am
I impatient—about some things. You'll be as safe in
France as you are here. When I make love to you, it
will be because you want it as much as I do.'

'Then that will be *never*! You'll be wasting your

time,' she cut in swiftly, but even as she said the words it was as though she was only saying what she felt she must. The strangest things were happening to her—a fine inner tremor, a warmth she didn't understand, a sense of weakness in her legs, as though she could hardly stand. She didn't like this man, because of all he was, and had done, but never could she deny his power to manipulate. She felt, for the first time in her life, frightened.

He looked at her, and there was much in that glance she didn't understand. She went on quickly: 'You said once, when I accused you of taking over my life, that no one could do that, only if I let them—yet it's what you're trying to do now, isn't it? You're telling me what you're going to do—and it's——' She stopped, overwhelmed by the strength of her own emotion. She felt breathless, and vulnerable, and helpless. She shivered and rubbed her arms, and looked at him, and there was nothing of laughter or amusement in his eyes or face now, he was deadly serious. 'W-why don't you leave me alone?'

'Because something began when we met, something I don't understand either. But we both know it. Life changes all the time. We meet people, we travel, we talk, links are made, and broken, nothing remains static. For us, for both of us, nothing can ever be the same again. There's no going back. There never will be.' White-faced, she listened to his words, and when he had finished speaking he added: 'Now you know.' He turned and walked away from her, out of the room, and there was silence.

Arwenna put her hand to her mouth and pressed the knuckles against her lips. She tried desperately to think of James, but nothing came. She couldn't picture his face at all. She wondered if she was going mad.

CHAPTER FIVE

THE conversation might never have been. Garth's behaviour when they went out was different again. Impersonal, businesslike, he asked her what she had thought about the contents of the French folder, and she told him.

'Very astute,' he said, when she had finished. 'You must know France well.'

'Enough to see, once I'd made a few notes, that these properties more or less stretch in a curving line from Paris to Nice, but none of them on the main routes —the Routes Nationales.'

'No. Tourists miss a lot of the old France, the real country, in their efforts to get from A to B—or in most cases from Paris to the South.'

'But I'm still none the wiser as to why,' she said. 'I mean, you can't be planning to buy a whole series of châteaux and hotels in a line.'

Garth laughed. 'No, I'm not. But I'm going to look at as many as I can when we go. We'll drive from Paris and follow the old trails, and visit the hotels particularly, not as a prospective buyer but as a guest. A business friend of mine is planning a book of alternative places to stay in France, small, out-of-the-way places off the beaten track for the more discerning tourist. I can see his point, and it's a damned good idea, and it'll work.'

'One snag. If everyone starts to go to these places, they'll no longer be out-of-the-way and 'off the beaten track' as you put it. *They'll* become the in-places.'

'Not quite. It's a large country, and the scope is enormous. I'm just taking one aspect of it this time, but imagine a spider's web spread all over France, with small hotels all over the place, linked by minor roads instead of major ones—no, it'll work.'

'Is that what you do? Buy property?'

'Mainly. It's what I started out in when I was twenty, when houses were cheap. I worked up from a few to many—with a lot of hard work, and a stroke of good fortune at the right time.'

He looked at her across the dimly lit table of the small Italian restaurant. It was a corner table, in an alcove screened by trailing plants on a wooden trellis wall, and a red candle flickered in the Chianti bottle on the table, and they had eaten a delicious pasta, and were drinking a rosé wine. The restaurant was fairly crowded, but their corner was a quiet oasis in the desert of sound that swirled around nearby, not too near. It was nearly nine o'clock, and Arwenna felt tired after the events of the day, but she didn't want to go back, to be alone with Garth. 'You mean you just decided to go into property—why?'

'I'd worked on a building site for two years, and saved all I made. I'd also learnt plastering, carpentry, how to put in windows——' He held out his hands. 'Look at them. You can still see the scars—faded now, but there.' She looked. His hands were powerful and big, and she saw the old scars of callouses and cuts, marks that would probably never vanish, and he wasn't ashamed of them; he didn't need to be. 'So when I'd saved enough I bought a little terraced house in an unfashionable part of London—I'd studied the trends, and it seemed logical to me that the area was ripe for a takeover from the smart set—and I did the house up so that it was like new. The first couple who saw it when it was done bought it. I made enough on that one to buy two, equally derelict, in the same area. I worked an eighteen-hour day and slept in one of the houses, and paid a friend who was equally hard up but a good electrician to do the re-wiring. By the time I was twenty-four I'd renovated ten houses and was looking around for more, in areas where prices were right. I'd got three men helping me, all damned hard workers who were prepared to do a good day's work for their pay—and then I bought a semi-detached in a bad state, and set to do it myself.'

'There was an old chap living in the attached house and he did nothing but complain about the noise and the dust. He took me in to show me one morning after I'd spent a couple of days knocking out rotten cupboards, and he was quivering with indignation as he showed me the dirt my work had brought into his house.' He touched his glass thoughtfully. 'God, his house was a mess! How he could have told the difference between the dirt of years and the stuff I was supposed to have knocked through, I don't know. I was about to tell him so—fairly politely, when something made me stop. I looked round his living room. There was no carpet on the floor, just lino—worse than some I'd ripped out next door. He had a bed in one corner, no fire—and it was a bitter November day, and on the table were what looked like the remains of his breakfast, a stale crust and some margarine in the paper.

'I looked at him, and he wore gloves with no fingers —and he looked grey with cold. Only his indignation was keeping him going. I apologised profusely, assured him I'd do something about it, and the next day I went in just before lunchtime and told him I'd come to clean up. I took my Thermos of soup with me and my sandwiches—Bovril, I think they were.' He grinned very faintly at her. 'I spent as little as possible on myself in those days. I also took in a bucket of coal I'd dredged from my coalshed next door. I lit him a fire, asked him if he'd like to share my lunch, and began to sweep up. The poor old devil was desperately lonely. He told me his life story over the next two hours. Not a relative in the world, no hobbies—there wasn't even a book in the house—and only his stamp collection to look at. I expressed an interest in it, and we sat by a good fire and I looked through his album, and made him a cup of tea, and talked. I could have been working—I should have been getting on with repairs, but I didn't have the heart to leave him. Then I found a stamp that I thought might be valuable, and told him. You could almost see the suspicion flaring in his eyes, as though I was going to pinch it from him, so I suggested he write to any large philatelists and get it valued—in fact, I'd do it for him, I said.' He paused.

Arwenna, enthralled with the story, said impatiently: 'Was it valuable? What happened?'

'They gave him a fair price for it, about sixty pounds if I remember. I got to know him well in the weeks that followed, took him something to eat every day—it was the only hot meal he ever had, I suspect—and kept him going with fires. Then, when the job next door was nearly done, I felt a sense of obligation. He wasn't cantankerous when I got to know him, just old and lonely and poorly nourished. I got him fixed up with meals on wheels, left him with a good supply of coal that I'd bought, and promised to go and see him once a week. Then, one day in February, another bitter cold day, I went in and he was lying on the floor. He'd fallen and broken his hip. I got him into hospital and two months later he died there.' He gave a deep sigh. 'It was such a waste, a damned waste! If only I'd known before——'

'Known what?' she said, disturbed by his words, and saddened.

Garth looked at her, eyes bleak. 'A month after he died I received a solicitor's letter, asking me to call in. When I got there, they told me that old Mr Simpson had left everything to me in his Will.' He took a deep breath. 'Do you know what I thought? I thought it would be his stamp collection—I——' he paused, and closed his eyes, as though in pain. 'God, what a *waste!*'

'*What?*' she demanded urgently.

'He'd left me eighty thousand pounds. *Eighty thousand.* It was all in stocks and shares that he'd accumulated over the years and never touched, and the money had grown and grown—and he'd lived like a recluse, not touching it. He could have lived in luxury, with good food and heat—but he hadn't. I felt ill at first. The money just didn't sink in at all until later. Then, when I realised that I actually possessed that amount, I vowed I would make use of it—as a sort of tribute to him, if you like. I didn't feel as though it belonged to me—I'd done nothing to deserve it.'

'You'd befriended an old man, fed him, helped him, talked to him——'

'But not for that. I thought he was penniless. I felt sorry for him.'

'You were the only friend he had,' she said softly. 'That must have meant a lot.' She was seeing another aspect of Garth, a side of him that wasn't all hard and decisive. He was a man who had taken pity on a fellow human being, and in so doing reaped a reward far greater than anyone could have envisaged.

'That's what I told myself, and so I went ahead and did all the things I'd imagined would take me years to do. I took calculated risks, studied the trends in house moving, bought a block of flats—and never looked back.'

'The men who worked with you at first, what happened to them?' she asked.

'Mike, the electrician, is a director in one of my companies up north. The other two, Bob and Eddy, are here in London. You'll probably meet them soon. I never forget those who've helped me.'

Arwenna smiled faintly. 'I'm sure you don't.'

A waiter was hovering respectfully near, and Garth

beckoned him over. 'Do you want anything else to eat?' he asked her.

She shook her head. 'No, thanks.'

'Then I'll have the bill, please.' The waiter beamed and vanished, and Arwenna regarded Garth steadily.

'Are we going back to your apartment now?' she asked him.

'If you don't mind. I've a lot to catch up on.'

'Can I help you?'

'Do you want to? You don't have to work all day *and* all evening.'

'I'd like to.'

'Okay, fine.' He paid the bill and they went out into a cool summer's evening. It was still light, and the roads were busy. 'Shall we get a taxi or walk?' he asked her.

'Walk,' she answered promptly. The wine had left her rather lightheaded. She wasn't used to drinking much, and they had somehow consumed two bottles of a delightful rosé wine that had seemed very innocuous at the time, but whose effects she was now feeling.

'I don't want to worry you, but you're weaving about slightly,' said Garth, and took hold of her arm.

'Am I?' The pavement had seemed a little uneven to her sandalled feet. 'It was that wine. I thought it was harmless.'

'It is. At least,' he corrected himself, looking down at her, 'I thought it was.'

'It's not—you're not—trying to get me drunk, are you?' she asked suddenly.

He burst out laughing, a hearty laugh that made an old woman walking her dog look round, shocked-faced, and sniff disapprovingly before pulling her dog's lead sharply and moving away. 'To seduce you?' he said, when he could speak. 'You've been watching some corny old films, haven't you?'

Arwenna tried to pull her arm away, affronted at his laughter, but he tightened his grip. 'That's not my

way,' he said quietly, and steered her towards the curb
ready to cross.

'Then what is?' she demanded, still annoyed.

There was a gap in the traffic, and they walked
quickly across. 'I've never needed one,' he answered.

'Implying that women fling themselves at you?'

'I didn't say that,' he chided. 'You musn't read
things into what I say.'

'Well, they would, wouldn't they?' she said tartly.
'You've got pots of money.'

'Thanks.' His voice was dry.

'I'm tired of this conversation,' Arwenna sighed.

'You started it, accusing me.'

'Can I phone when we get back?' she asked.

'Of course. Let me guess. James?'

'Yes, my fiancé.' She stressed the last word.

'You've told him where you're staying? In case he
wants to phone you,' Garth added delicately.

'I—er—gave him the number. He didn't ask——'
she swallowed.

'Oh, would he be annoyed?'

'What the hell do *you* think?'

'He'd be annoyed,' he said gently.

'I'll tell him tonight.'

'Just as long as you feel strong enough——'

'What does that mean?' she asked crossly.

He shrugged. 'You know him better than I do. Do
you ever have rows?'

'That's none of your business!'

They were rounding the corner, nearing the block of
flats in which Garth lived, and a Rolls-Royce was just
drawing away from the front entrance.

The driver tooted, and Garth raised his free hand in
salute. It vanished round the corner. 'I should imagine
you do, myself, being of such different temperaments.'

'I didn't ask you,' she said pertly, and ran up the
steps of the main door. He followed her in, towards the

lift, and the hall porter came out from behind his counter, waving two envelopes.

'Mr Vanner, sir,' he called. 'Couple of messages for you.'

'Thanks, Fred.' Garth took them from him, and put them in his jacket pocket. The lift shot upwards, and Arwenna realised something rather belatedly. The lift had only one button: it said 'Penthouse'. It hadn't occurred to her before, because the doorman had ushered her into it when she had come in that afternoon, and pressed the button for her. There were two other lifts in the spacious hall, and she could easily have got in one of those.

'Is this your private lift?' she asked.

'Yes.'

'Just for *you*?'

'Yes. The other lifts finish at the floor below.'

'Good gracious,' commented Arwenna. 'That's a bit posh, isn't it?' They had come to a halt, and the doors slid open. 'What happens if there's a fire?'

'Sensible question. You obviously haven't looked round. I'll show you.' He took her down the private hallway and opened a door. 'Stairs, leading directly down to the hall, bypassing the other floors. There's also a fire escape from outside my bedroom.'

'Burglars? If you can get down, they could get up,' she pointed out.

'Not with the alarms, they couldn't. I've got the latest electronic system installed. As you may have noticed, I have some antiques—I don't intend to let anyone help themselves. I've worked for all I have.'

'You let me into your apartment—and left me alone there. Weren't you bothered?' she asked, as they went into the apartment.

He looked at her as if faintly shocked. 'I didn't think for a moment about it.'

Which meant that he trusted her. It gave Arwenna

a warm feeling. But would she have trusted him if the positions were reversed? She suddenly thought, *I would trust him with my life*. And it was a strange thought to have, in the light of their previous conversation. She watched him as he walked away from her towards the drinks cupboard. With my life, with my life—the aftertaste of the realisation lingered, and it was true. It was also very disturbing. Something was happening to Arwenna that she didn't fully understand.

Garth had his back to her, at the cupboard. 'Why don't you go and telephone James while I'm fixing a drink?'

'Yes, I will. Nothing strong for me, please. Not if I'll be working. I need a clear head.'

He didn't turn around. 'A lot of orange juice and a little gin?'

'Perfect.' She ran up the steps, went through the doorway, and into her bedroom. She took a deep breath before dialling James' number. It was quite clear, when he answered, that he was annoyed, but was trying hard to control it.

'Where've you been?' he asked. 'I tried you last night—I've tried you half a dozen times today and again this evening and there was nothing, no reply— what kind of hotel is this, for heaven's sake?'

'Ah!' Now was the time for the truth, and it suddenly wasn't easy. 'I'm not at a hotel, James darling,' she said. 'Actually, this is Garth's *huge* apartment, and——'

'What?' His voice quivered. 'His *apartment*? You mean you're staying with *him*?'

'It's only round the corner from the clinic, love— hotels are hard to——'

'You're staying there with *him*? Who else is there?'

This was not going easily. 'No one,' she answered. 'Don't you trust me, James?'

There was such a long pause that she thought they

had been cut off, then: 'I don't trust *him*,' he snapped. He wasn't annoyed any more, he was furiously angry. 'How the hell do you think I feel?'

'I know how you feel,' she answered. 'But let me remind you, it was your invitation to dinner that started all this.'

'I wondered how long it would be before you threw that at me,' he snapped. 'It didn't give you a licence to share his flat—and his bed, for all I——'

'Take that back!' she cut in. 'How *dare* you!'

'I dare. He's a real smoothie, right? And worth pots of money——'

Arwenna slammed the receiver down furiously, shaking with anger. 'Damn, damn, damn!' she muttered, and stood up. Still furious, she stalked into the main room and glared at Garth, who was holding a glass out.

'Your drink,' he said. 'Everything okay back at the ranch?'

'Cut out the sarcasm,' she snapped. She gave him a look that should have withered him, and he winced.

'Ouch! Something wrong?'

'Nothing's wrong. Everything's *perfect*. Why should anything be wrong?' she demanded.

'Because you look to me as though you'd like to stick a knife in someone—preferably me. Or could it be James?' There was no trace of laughter on his face, but it was in his eyes; amusement glinted, betraying him. He handed her the glass, not standing too near, as though frightened she might hit him.

She drank it all in one go, then gasped. 'Ah,' said Garth. 'I was just going to tell you—I'd only added a little orange. I was going to ask you to say when with it.' He produced a small jug of orange juice as if to give truth to his words, and managed to look apologetic. It didn't fool Arwenna for one moment. If he dared even smile, he'd be sorry. Just the merest flicker.

'Very amusing,' she said, when she had drawn a

much-needed breath. 'Very, very fun——' The shrill
ring of the telephone cut off her words. Garth looked
at her, one eyebrow raised questioningly.

'James?' he queried.

'Most likely.'

'Do you want to?' He gestured towards the ringing
telephone. Far better that she should answer it than he.
She walked over and picked it up.

'Hello,' she said. A woman's voice came, not James'.

'Hello?' It was a puzzled word. 'Is Garth there?'

'Yes. Just a moment, please.' Arwenna held out the
receiver. 'For you,' she said.

He took it from her. 'Hello, Vanner here.' Then,
after a pause during which Arwenna could hear the
faint voice at the other end: 'A friend. Yes, staying here.
Yes. No, I'm sorry, Paula, not for several days—yes,
fine. I'll ring you as soon as I——' There was another
long pause as he listened. Arwenna added orange juice
to her glass and sipped it slowly. She was gradually
calming down, not sure whom to be more annoyed with,
James, Garth, or herself for slamming the phone down
before. He had every right to be furious. She probably
would have been, in his place.

The call was over. He replaced the receiver, face expressionless. 'Another lady friend?' she enquired sarcastically.

'Yes.' He picked up his glass. 'Ready for work?'

'There's nothing else to do, is there?' she answered.

'You could phone James back. You did hang up on
him, didn't you?'

'How did you know that?'

'I went to the kitchen for the orange juice. I couldn't
help overhearing it slam down.'

'I suppose you were listening as well?' she accused.

'I wouldn't dream of it,' he replied blandly. 'Mind
you, now you mention it, I did hear you demanding
that he take something back.'

'My God, you must have walked quickly to get back here after——'

'True.' He gave a modest smile. 'I'm a very fast mover.' He paused, as though to let the double-edged words sink in, then added: 'Had he insulted you?'

'Not so's you'd notice. Just accused me of sharing your bed,' she snapped.

Garth poured some gin into her glass, almost absentmindedly it seemed, and Arwenna watched him do it without realizing fully what he *was* doing. 'Good grief. That wasn't very nice——'

'Perhaps he knows you better than I,' she said.

'Perhaps. But he should also know you far better than he knows me. He should surely trust you——'

'He does!'

'It doesn't sound like it. Tell me, when he was pursuing you hotly all over Europe, proposing to you, did he have any cause to worry then?'

Arwenna really didn't know why she was standing here talking to him. The subject should have been closed before—but it was difficult, with him. 'You mean was I running round with Frenchmen and Italians?' she said scornfully. 'Don't be ridiculous! I was working, remember? I'd not have kept my job long if I'd been gadding about.'

He regarded her very levelly. 'You must have had time off. And I did see you at the party last night. You weren't doing so badly for yourself.'

'I didn't think you'd noticed.' She laughed. 'Being chatted up, you mean? Mmm, that was fun—before that green-eyed bitch of yours tried to assault me.'

'She's not my green-eyed bitch any more. I already apologised for that. Do you always have men following you wherever you go?'

'All the time,' she answered. He'd be sorry he'd asked in a minute. 'All right, I admit it. I had a *marvellous* time abroad. Of course I had time off, and I

made the most of it. Do you want a list of my lovers?'
She frowned. 'If I can remember their names, that is.
Let's see, there was Henri, he was a Belgian diplomat
in Paris, very charming, we had a glorious weekend in
Brussels——'

Garth wasn't looking amused any more. His eyes
were very hard and cold. 'All right,' he said. 'Joke's
over——'

'It's no joke,' she said, enjoying herself. 'He proposed to me in bed! Now there's an original place for
a proposal, isn't it?' It was true—but not in the way
she intended him to take it. Henri had indeed proposed,
and *he* had been in bed with 'flu on a very respectable
visit to his family in Brussels. 'And then there was
Philippe—French, very wealthy—let me see, we had a
super fling when my family went off for a few days——'
She gave a throaty chuckle. Philippe had indeed been
French, and wealthy, and he and Arwenna had spent
several days in the same house when the family who
employed her had gone away to visit a sick grand-
mother—leaving their children with Arwenna. And
they had had a glorious, fun-filled time, because
Philippe, a cousin of Madame la Roche, her employer,
was fantastic with the children and had tired them out
all day, devising new and original games for them to
play. He was also only twelve, and his mother had left
him in Arwenna's care while she too visited Grand'-
mère.

'I get the picture,' said Garth dryly. 'Please spare me
any——'

'You asked,' she countered.

'True.' He took a swallow of his vodka and tonic as
though he needed it. 'But I didn't want a blow-by-blow
account of your affairs.'

Arwenna began to laugh, glorious deep-throated
laughter. If only he knew the truth! 'Then shall we
begin work?' she suggested.

'Perhaps we'd better.' Garth put down his glass. 'I'll go and get the papers I need.' And he walked away. Arwenna watched him go. Something had annoyed him. Why she had spoken so outrageously, she would never know. It was totally out of character for her to do so—yet it was all a part of the other things she didn't understand about herself—and equally disturbing to her.

She bit her lip, suddenly unsure of herself, and went to the table near the window, and began to tidy the folders there, ready for Garth's return.

It was morning. She had slept dreadfully, and awoke with the sensation of having a terrible hangover. Groaning, she sat up in bed and put her hand to her head. Then, realising the time, she jumped out, pulled on her dressing gown, and went into the kitchen.

Garth sat there, eating toast, fully dressed. 'It's after nine,' she gasped.

'I know. Good morning, Arwenna,' he responded calmly.

'Good morning.'

'Do you want toast?'

'Yes, I'll do it.' She found the bread and popped two slices in the toaster.

'There was no point in waking you before. They're not operating until nine-thirty. I've been on the phone to Bill Chisholm, and all is fine. Your aunt had a comfortable night. They'll phone us when she comes round, and tell you when you can visit her.'

Arwenna took a deep breath. 'Thanks,' she said. 'I know it's silly, but—I'm shaky, now that it's going to happen——' She bit her lip. 'She's very dear to me.'

'I know, and she's in excellent hands. She's also a remarkably fit woman for her age, Arwenna. There's nothing to worry about. Sit down, I'll butter your toast. Pour yourself a cup of coffee.'

She obediently sat, and a few moments later Garth handed her her toast. 'Now eat up, then go and get dressed, and we'll do some more work. Easy stuff. You worked damned well last night, no wonder you slept on.'

She *had* worked hard the previous evening, they both had. Until past midnight, and the time had passed incredibly swiftly once they had begun. With Garth's words still resting uneasy in her mind, and her own confusion about her reaction, Arwenna had found it far easier to concentrate on the folder in French, and in the translation of it, and her mind had been sharpened accordingly, while he had made notes, asked pertinent questions, until there was another detailed folder, in English, on the table. He wrote quickly, and his sharp brain had stimulated Arwenna's, had exhilarated her. He was a challenge in himself, and when the work was done at last, and he had gone to make them both coffee, she had sat back and thought about the evening. She was tired, but it was the satisfying tiredness that comes only after stimulating work, and it had made her realise something about herself. She had never been so mentally pushed before, in any of her jobs. Some part of her had come alive. She had known then that in spite of everything, Garth's 'blackmail', his reasons for getting her to work for him, she was going to enjoy her work for him.

She looked at him now. 'The Italian folder?' she queried.

'No. There's much more planning to be done for our French trip—or had you forgotten that?'

'How could I?' she countered.

A slight twitching of his mouth betrayed amusement. 'Then you can plan our itinerary, where we'll stay, etcetera. You've read enough to know which are the places that should be most interesting to me—or should do. It'll be interesting to see if our ideas coincide.'

'You're putting a lot of confidence in my judgment, aren't you?' she answered. 'I'm not a property expert.'

'You're a woman who's travelled a lot. So see yourself as a holidaymaker, a tourist. Base your plans on those lines. It is, after all, the tourists *I'm* concerned about. I work on a different wavelength—you will be my link, if you like.'

'With ordinary people? Thanks!' she said dryly.

'You *know* what I mean.' His voice had a sharper edge to it. 'We don't need to beat about the bush with each other any more, Arwenna. Not after last night.' His eyes were dark upon her and she couldn't look away. 'I told you, we're two of a kind. And after several hours working with you, I was even more convinced of it. Don't underestimate yourself——'

'I don't,' she cut in sharply.

'Then don't pick me up on words when you know damned well what I mean.'

She accepted the reprimand with a slight smile—a rueful smile, and Garth stood up. 'I'll go and get everything ready. Do you prefer to work in the lounge, or in the study?'

'The lounge.'

'Right. I'll be ready when you are.' He walked out, leaving her to finish her coffee.

Fifteen minutes later they had begun the morning's work, and it was different, but connected with their previous night's work, and gradually a picture began to emerge of what would soon be happening, and Arwenna found herself so totally absorbed in the plans that she was scarcely aware of the passage of time.

The telephone shrilled, and she dropped her pen and looked at him.

He stood up. 'I'll get it.' Arwenna looked at her watch. It was nearly twelve, and she heard him speaking, heard his voice, and her mouth was dry. Then she saw him nod, look across at her, and he raised his hand

and gave her the thumbs-up sign. He was smiling.

She stood, suddenly shaky, her eyes filling with tears, her mouth quivering. Garth put the telephone down and walked across to her, and held her arms with his strong warm hands. 'She's fine,' he said. 'Fine and dandy. Came round from the anaesthetic about half an hour ago and went straight to sleep again.'

Arwenna tried to laugh, and it came out as a sob. Garth put his arms round her, gently, but very decisively. 'Don't cry, you cuckoo,' he scolded. 'We can go and see her soon.'

'I'm not crying,' her voice was muffled, leaning as she was against his chest. She felt her hair being stroked, and she felt very safe and sheltered, and warm. There was no question of her trying to move away. Just for the moment it seemed right for her to be there. 'I'm just so—happy and relieved that it's all over. Thank you Garth.' She lifted her face to look at him, and gave a tremulous smile. 'Thank you.'

She saw his eyes darken, felt his hold tighten fractionally, saw his mouth, and it was a warm, sensuous mouth. He had probably kissed, and been kissed by, many women, and she knew why, and she wanted him to kiss her, and suddenly it wasn't right for her to be there any more. She moved; she made a little sound in her throat and tried to move away, only she couldn't.

Then he put his hand at the back of her head, his fingers pressing into the tumble of deep auburn curls, and his mouth came down on hers in a long, lingering, beautiful kiss.

CHAPTER SIX

THEN it was over, and Arwenna wasn't sure whether it had lasted a second or a lifetime. She only knew that no kiss had ever been so complete and wonderful. Shakily, as Garth released her—reluctantly, it seemed—she stepped away from him, eyes bright now not with tears but with something else, and he reached out and touched her under her chin, lifting her face slightly, making her look at him.

'Thank *you*,' he said softly. 'It was just as I imagined it would be.'

'You shouldn't have——' she began.

'No, how true. You're an engaged lady. Very naughty of me, I know.' His eyes held hers, and there was a depth of excitement there. Not laughter, not any more, but something so different that the very air in the room seemed to shimmer with an unknown brightness, and everything else was very still. 'But you see, I've been wanting to kiss you for a long time—and I always do what I want, sooner or later.' He took his fingers away from beneath her chin, not abruptly, but with the trace of a lingering caress. 'And I took advantage of you too.' His mouth was touched with the faintest smile. 'I shall apologise to your aunt when we visit her—mentally, of course, because she wouldn't understand why—but I won't apologise to you.'

Arwenna took a deep breath, but before she could speak, he added: 'And now I'm going to order some flowers for us to take. Will you be good enough to make us both a cup of coffee—or tea—whichever pleases you?'

She turned away and walked from him, released, and heard him pick up the telephone. She was supposed to be annoyed, and she didn't know why she wasn't. She didn't know what she felt, but she was faintly disturbed, and much confused.

When she returned with two cups of coffee Garth was sitting down by the table again. He looked up at her. 'Thanks, we'll leave when the flowers arrive,' he told her. 'We'll walk there. Then, after our visit, we'll come back here. Any questions?'

'Then what? Are you going out or working here?'

'What do you prefer?'

She shrugged, watched him light a thin cigar. He smiled. 'Sorry. You don't mind me smoking, do you?'

'Of course not.'

'I said, what do you prefer?'

'You must know what you have to do today,' she retorted. 'I don't. There's quite a lot for me to do here, as you know.'

'Yes, I know. I think we'll take a trip to my office after visiting your aunt, collect some papers I need, then work here for the rest of today. It's sensible, for if your aunt needs you, and we can visit her later, when she's fully recovered. They did ask me to tell you that you may find her very sleepy when we go—but it's perfectly natural.'

'Yes, I'm prepared for that,' she nodded. Perhaps she had imagined the kiss. She began to wonder if she had. And what was a kiss, after all? Nothing of any sort of significance.

The telephone shrilled and Garth rose to answer it, spoke briefly, and put it down.

'The florists have just delivered downstairs,' he said. 'When we've finished our coffee, we'll go.'

Arwenna kissed her aunt's cheek. The old lady lay in bed with eyes closed, but she stirred slightly at Arwenna's movement and murmured something unintelligible.

'The nurse says we can only stay for a moment or two,' she whispered to the sleeping woman, not sure if her words could be understood or not. 'But we'll call again later to see you.'

There was no response, save a slight sigh, and Arwenna kissed her cheek again and tiptoed to the door.

Outside, Garth was talking to a tall grey-haired attractive man who smiled warmly at Arwenna and shook her hand as he introduced them. 'Hello, Arwenna,' said Bill Chisholm. 'I was just telling Garth that your aunt's fine. The operation was quite straight-forward, and all being well, I'll have her home in a week.'

'Thank you very much, Mr Chisholm, we're very grateful.' She smiled at him.

'Anything for Garth.' He grinned at him. 'I've told him, any time he needs his appendix whipping out, he's only to ask.'

Garth laughed. 'Thanks. I'll keep what I have. I know you butchers!'

'Ssh!' Bill Chisholm looked around in mock alarm. 'Don't let the patients hear you. *They* trust me.'

Garth clapped him on the shoulder. 'Only because of your smooth bedside manner, you old fraud——' Arwenna listened, amused. The two were clearly old friends. There was a camaraderie about them that came only from mutual respect and affection.

She suddenly realised that she was being spoken to. She had, for a brief moment, been remembering a kiss...

'Sorry?' she said.

'Bill's asking us if we'd like to go round tomorrow evening for a drink?' said Garth, looking amused, as if he guessed her thoughts.

'Oh, how kind.' She looked at Garth for guidance, and he nodded.

'We'll be delighted. What time? Eightish?' he said.

'Yes, fine. Anne will be glad to see you again. Lovely. See you then.' A bleeper sounded from his pocket, and he pulled a face. 'Duty calls. You can find your way out?' He took Arwenna's hand and shook it. 'Nice to have met you, Arwenna. Don't worry about your aunt. Despite Garth's vile slanderous remarks, for which I shall possibly sue him, she's being very well looked after, I promise you. See you tomorrow evening?'

'Yes, I look forward to it. Goodbye.'

Walking out into the warm summer's day, she asked: 'Have you known him long?'

'About eight years. I sold him his house—I think you'll like it. His wife's very charming, and they've got three kids, the youngest of whom I'm godfather to.' He looked at her. 'He doesn't invite just anyone round for drinks, either. You must appeal to him.'

'I liked him very much,' she said, warmed by the compliment.

'You'd get on with most of my friends, I imagine,' he went on. 'Do you get on with James' friends?'

'Of course I——' she stopped, and looked sharply at him. 'What do you mean?'

He shrugged. 'It's a perfectly simple question. Do you?'

'Yes, of course.' She was suddenly annoyed at the implications. And oddly, more so because she couldn't stand some of James' friends—but had no intention of telling Garth that. She added, with a touch of asperity: 'And none have ever attacked me.'

'I asked for that, I suppose.' He took her arm as they dodged across the busy road. 'Aren't you ever going to let me forget it?'

She smiled sweetly. 'I don't know. It all depends——'

'On my questions about James? Okay. I don't like him and you don't like Marcia. And I got rid of

Marcia——' the rest of the sentence didn't need to be said. Arwenna shook his hand off her arm as they neared the car park beneath the flats.

'So you did,' she said softly. 'And you have no reason to dislike James——'

'I have plenty,' he cut in 'But there's only one reason that counts.'

'I don't want to know what it is,' she said, and walked on, sandalled feet clicking over cement, walking towards his car. Garth caught up with her and took hold of her arm.

'Because you already know,' he said.

Arwenna turned to face him by the car. No one else was about. There were few cars in, and vast empty spaces. It was a lonely place, a quiet place, and she wouldn't like to be alone there at night. 'Because I'm engaged to him, and going to marry him,' she said.

'You're engaged. You're not going to marry him,' he answered. They were standing only a foot apart, and it was shadowy there, away from the light slanting in, and there were solid concrete pillars near them, and a silence, the distant traffic muted, and there was a fine thread of tension reaching out to touch and fill them. Garth seemed, because of the shadows, to be even bigger and he wasn't laughing; he wasn't even amused. He was dark and serious—and his face was very hard.

Arwenna felt herself shiver slightly, and it seemed to have gone cold. 'Yes—yes, I am,' she said, and her beautiful eyes, so dark-lashed, normally so calm, were angry. 'Yes,' she repeated, 'I love him.'

'Love? You don't know what love is,' he grated. 'You were attracted to him, and he pursued you, made you feel wanted——'

'You're a liar,' she snapped, wishing she didn't feel so very cold. 'You have no right to say things when you know nothing!'

He suddenly took hold of her hand, not gently, and

shook her as if angry. 'I don't have to know *him* to know that,' he said urgently. 'My God, you'd waste your life if you were fool enough——'

'I've *heard* enough!' Incensed, she struggled to free herself from his grip. 'How dare you hold me—talk to me like——'

She was silenced by his mouth as it came down on hers, blotting out her words in a savage kiss that was raw in its intensity and deep in its excitement. Her senses swam, reeling under the strength of it; she would have fallen had his hands not held her so firmly. She fought blindly to free herself, and then—and then suddenly she wasn't struggling any more, but finding her treacherous body responding against her will to the drugging sensation of overwhelming, trembling sensuality. As his hands moved, one across her back, the other to her waist, to secure his hold, she knew an all-encompassing inner warmth that she couldn't any longer deny.

Sensed blurred, completely overwhelmed, she gave herself up to the moment, and their bodies, touching so closely, were almost as one. She could feel Garth's heartbeats, rapid and strong, and was aware of her own heart hammering in unison. It was as if nothing else existed, and as if time had ceased to her. There was no cold any more, only a fire which swept through her.

'Oh God,' whispered Garth, and he was trembling as he held her, and she realised that the kiss, the love-making in an embrace, was over. He held her still, as if he was never going to let her go, and he was like a man with a fever, an uncontrollable surging fever that filled him too. His mouth was touching her hair. His warm breath teased it, his arms had a fine tremor that filled her because of the strength of him, and because it was in her too. She couldn't have moved even had she wanted to, and she no longer wanted to. There was no strength in her, no resistance at all, and she realised that her arms were around him, clinging to him, yet she was not aware of having put them there. Then at last, after eons of time, Garth moved, opened the car door, pushed her in, got in the other side and closed the doors, and reached towards her blindly.

Some slight vestige of reason remained. The seconds of moving into the car had allowed her a breathing space, literally and figuratively, and Arwenna made a slight sound of protest and tried to lift her hand to push him away, but it was not enough, and she was not strong enough—— Gently, this time, like a man for whom there is nothing save one thought, he kissed her again, and held her face as he kissed her eyes, her cheeks, her nose, then, at last, her mouth.

This time, lost to all reason, Arwenna gave herself fully to the sweet heady sensation of his seeking mouth, and the kiss was like none she had ever known before in her life. It was unutterably beautiful, and it was gentle, and they were in a dark, shadowy, wonderful place where no one existed save them. Garth's hands, warm and equally gentle, traced the soft contours of her body in featherlight caress that only served to give the kiss an added dimension, a depth. There was no reason in her any more. All was touch, and sensation, and a deep, deep warmth, and a knowledge that went beyond time, beyond anything she had ever known before.

Then, gradually, and because perfection must be brief, or it is no longer perfect, they drew away from each other, and he looked at her, and there was an urgent tremor that still touched him, but she couldn't see him properly because she was too dazed, and for a few moments they were motionless, and silent, because no words could be said. He reached out to stroke her cheek, and his hand was trembling, and she made a soft murmur as he touched her mouth with his fingers, and closed her eyes.

She heard him take a deep breath, heard his sigh. She couldn't move. She didn't want to open her eyes, she was still drugged, almost drowsy, but she did so, at last, and he was still watching her. It was very shadowy in the car, but she could see his face, dark, tanned, and he had what seemed to be lines of pain, a drawn look, and his mouth was slightly open, and he ran his tongue over his lips as she looked at him. Then he reached up and rubbed his face, as if waking up from a deep sleep.

Arwenna felt her strength returning, and with it came a realisation of what had just happened, and that was followed by a kind of self-loathing, a contempt for her own weakness.

She had just allowed—not only allowed, revelled in —Garth's embraces and lovemaking, and she had responded to him with shameful abandon, all thoughts of fidelity to James completely forgotten as though he hadn't even existed. And this was the man who had told her he would make love to her, a man who had forced her to work for him, a man of strong personality and now, apparently, equally strong passions, who always got what he wanted—and he wanted Arwenna. If she hadn't believed it before, she did now. She sat there very still, as the deeper realisations and implications of what had just taken place washed over her. If Garth had decided to test her loyalty to James, he had chosen his method very carefully, and with great skill. He had told her that she was safe, staying in his flat with him, but how could she be sure of that now? She couldn't. She had betrayed not only James, but herself, and she wasn't sure which was worse. She only knew that she felt dreadful—as though she had been used. She turned to look at him, and she saw him clearly now, and it seemed to her that there might have been a faint look of triumph in his eyes, a sureness, a knowing. She felt sick.

'I hope you're pleased with yourself,' she said, and her voice held all the bitterness she was feeling.

'Pleased?' He repeated the word as if he didn't understand it.

'You—you——' She had to pause to calm herself. 'You did that deliberately!'

'Kissed you?'

'Made me respond,' she answered. 'My God, you must have had lots of practice!'

He hit the steering wheel hard with the edge of his hand. 'What the hell do you want me to say? That you're the first woman I've kissed? No, you're not. Did I *imagine* that you enjoyed it? What's the matter? Suffering pangs of conscience? I won't tell James, if that's what you're worried about.'

'No, that's not what I'm worried about,' she shot back. 'I'm staying in *your* flat—sleeping there——' She was shaking.

'And you think that after this, I'm going to be creeping into your room?'

'Yes, damn you! Do you blame me?' She flashed, eyes shining with unshed tears. 'And we're going to France——'

'I've already told you, you're safe.'

'And I don't believe you. Not after that skilful piece of——' she stopped, bit her lip.

'I kissed you because I wanted to kiss you more than anything else,' he answered, and the air crackled with tension. 'Not because I'd plotted to do so—what do you think I am? A bloody computer, working out every move? I'm a *man*——'

'I know that!' she interrupted. 'You made that very clear. And you want to make love to me—yes, you've made that equally clear—well, I don't want to make love to you!'

'That wasn't the impression I had five minutes ago,'

he said, and his eyes were dark and angry, and a muscle moved in his jaw, and he searched her face as if not believing what he was hearing.

Arwenna struck out blindly at him, fist clenched, sobbing, and caught his cheek a hard blow, but he took her wrist and held it, and pulled it away from his face, then caught her other hand roughly. 'You'll hear me,' he grated, voice shaking with anger. 'You wanted me——'

'*No!*'

'You wanted me,' he went on relentlessly, 'and you know it. And, if we hadn't been here it wouldn't have stopped where it did.'

He pulled her hands as she struggled, shaking her head, crying: 'No—no!'

'Oh yes,' he said. 'So why fight your own instincts? You *want* me as much as I want you.'

She was sobbing helplessly, hurting, aching, knowing the truth of his words, and because they were true, frightened. 'Leave me alone!' she cried, when she could speak. 'I hate you—I *hate* you!'

'And yourself, for being a woman,' he said. 'If you hate me, you must hate yourself as well, because I didn't mistake your response.'

He let her go, and held the steering wheel tightly as if he would like to break it, as if he would like to break her. Arwenna sat very still, exhausted, frightened at the controlled violence she sensed in him that filled the car. Garth turned to her, still holding the wheel as if he didn't trust himself to let it go. She saw a mark beneath his eye, a swelling of the skin, the beginning of a bruise, and she had done that, and was filled with a kind of horror at her own violence. He touched it, as if sensing her eyes on it, and said: 'I'll have a black eye tomorrow. I hope that pleases you.'

'I'm sorry,' she began. 'I didn't mean——'

'Think nothing of it,' he said crushingly. 'I'm sure

it gave you some satisfaction to hit me—if only to stop me saying what you couldn't bear to hear. I'm tired of this discussion. Are you ready to leave?'

'No, I'm not. I don't want to go to your office. I want to go——' She stopped. Where did she want to go? To his apartment? Where could she go? She was tied to him as though with invisible cords, her obligations too great to be broken. There was no escape from him. Not yet. Not until her debt was paid.

'I don't feel well,' she said, and that was no lie. She didn't want to face anyone, she felt weak and sick with all that had happened.

Garth opened his door, got out, closed and locked it. Then he walked round, opened her door and said : 'Get out, Arwenna.'

Silently she obeyed. He locked that too, then he took her arm as though she were a child and walked across towards the lift with her.

Minutes later, in his apartment, he said, 'Sit down. I'll make you a cup of tea. You'll feel better then.'

'But I don't want——'

'Sit down,' he ordered, steely, cold, hard. 'Please don't argue. I am not a patient man, and I don't feel very kindly towards you at this moment, owing to the fact that I have a headache, and a pain in my face, from your ladylike fist, and I would appreciate it if you just sat quietly for a while.' And he walked away from her and towards his kitchen.

Arwenna sat by the window, and looked out towards the clinic where her aunt lay recovering from her operation, blissfully—and fortunately—unaware of what was happening.

He returned with two beakers and sat down near her on the settee. 'Drink that,' he said. 'I've got the mother and father of a headache, and I'd prefer not to have any more arguments with you at the moment. I hope I make myself clear?'

She nodded. He hardly needed to tell her that he
wanted no more argument. She was in no state to do
so either. She was tired; she was tired of being independent, and strong, looking after everyone with whom
she came in contact. She wanted to be cosseted and
protected: she wanted someone to look after her. On
her shoulders rested the responsibility for Aunt Daisy's
operation—that was a burden she accepted willingly,
and with love. But there was the other, greater one. If
she backed out now, James' father would almost certainly go bankrupt. She leaned back into the cushioned
comfort of the settee and looked blindly at the ceiling,
seeing nothing save blurred white.

I'm tired, she thought, weary of the responsibility,
and he—Garth—is ruthless, wearing me down, giving
me nowhere to turn, nowhere to go to be safe, and free.
She knew there was an element of self-pity in her
thoughts, and it was alien to her, but just for the moment, she was incapable of doing anything about it.
There was work to be done, much work, waiting for
her; and travel abroad—a chance she knew many would
be delighted to have. She had no illusions about that.
Garth was an attractive man, wealthy, with a strong
decisive personality; none of those things could be
denied. And he had taken over her life, subtly and
gradually, and was still doing so. She resented the
fact, and him. She wanted to be cosseted, yes, but not
in this way. Not in the way that said, look at me—do as
I say or else. She wanted James to do it, to phone her,
to say, never mind Garth and my father, let *them* sort
it out between them, it's nothing to do with you. She
wondered what she would do if he rang now, and told
her that, and at the thought she almost smiled. Almost,
not quite.

Her head ached too, a dull persistent throbbing that
was getting worse. She sat up and drank her tea, then
realised that Garth had been sitting still, watching her.

'What have you been thinking?' he asked.

'You said you didn't want any more arguments,' she answered.

'Would it cause one?'

She nodded, winced as her head throbbed in protest, and said: 'I'm afraid so. I'm sorry, I'm not strong enough either. Let's leave it. Why did you ask, anyway?' She didn't really want to know, but she said it.

'You had a whole range of expressions chasing across your face,' he told her, and his voice was taut. He sat, not relaxed, not tense either, but watchful, wary, and she sensed that he had spoken the truth before. He was not a patient man. Something had happened to him that was as alien to him as self-pity was to Arwenna. Perhaps he found it as difficult to cope with as she did.

'I was just thinking—about life,' she answered. 'I've a headache too.'

'Mine's gone.'

'Well, bully for you!' She finished her tea and put the beaker on the table. 'Haven't you got lots of things to do? I'll work here while you're out. I will work, I promise.' Please go, she added, beneath her breath. Please go, because I don't know what's happening to me and I wish I did. I wish I could go to bed and lie down and cover my head and let the world pass by without me for a day or two. She wanted to cry, but she wasn't going to do that.

Garth lit a cheroot. 'I told you, I thought—that I'd deliberately kept this day free of outside work.'

'Oh. I'd forgotten.' There was a tiny thread loose in the heavy gold of the settee, and she picked at it with her nail; she didn't want to look at him any more.

'What are you doing?'

She looked up then, because it sounded from his voice as if he might be frowning, and he was. 'I'm sorry, it's just a thread——' She patted it back into place, and he stood up.

'For God's sake, don't start apologising every time
I speak!'

'I'm not. What do you want me to say?' He was
standing there, towering over her, but she wasn't going
to jump to her feet. 'That I'm pulling your stupid settee
to bits?' She shook her head. 'I thought you didn't
want any more arguments. It does seem as though that
might be slightly impossible, though, doesn't it?' She
glared at him angrily, and had a feeling almost of satisfaction at the darkening bruise beneath his left eye. 'Just
tell me what you'd like me to talk about and I'll try and
oblige. I am, after all, an *employee* of yours—and I'll
try not to forget that.'

Garth pulled her to her feet, reached forward, jerked
her upwards with both hands and held her, his face
dark with anger. For one moment it seemed that he
might strike her, but she stood her ground, unafraid,
ready to give as good as she got, weary of him, and of
nearly everyone—even James.

Her eyes flashed angrily. 'Go on,' she snapped, 'I
dare you!' Her body tensed.

'Dare me to what?'

'Hit me. It's what you want to do, isn't it? It's what
you've been itching to do ever since I struck you in the
car.'

'Don't be stupid!' he snarled, took his arms from her
arms, and turned away as if disgusted. 'Is that what you
thought? Is that the kind of man you know—the sort
that knock women about?'

'No, but you're different from any man I've ever met.
I've never known anyone with such explosive violence
inside them.'

'I don't hit *women*,' he grated. 'I never have. I certainly don't intend to start with you. What do you mean
—*violence*?' He turned his head, tilted it slightly as if
not believing what he had heard.

'It's there, in you—I can almost see it, feel it—

crackling tension—frightening——' She shivered, and held her arms to her as if for protection.

'Then if you see it, it must be because *you* bring it out. I am not a violent man.'

'You *were*! Years ago, you were,' she shot back, and realised, too late, that she had said what should never have been said. Garth went white, as if she had struck him, wounded him, and she wanted to take the words back, but it was too late for that. Perhaps it had been too late during that moment of their first meeting.

Then suddenly the air went very still, as if waiting for what was to come. In those next few moments Arwenna saw everything around her with great clarity as if it might be etched on her brain for ever.

She wanted to cry out, no, no, let me take it back, but it was too late. It had always been too late...

'I see,' he said. 'Perhaps you'd better finish what you started.' He spoke softly, almost sadly it seemed. 'Perhaps you'd better tell me exactly what you mean.'

She shook her head. 'I can't.'

'Then *I* had better tell *you*. It concerns when I lived in Raneley, years ago, as a young man, when you were a child.' He walked slowly away from her, towards the window. There he turned. 'Doesn't it?'

'It's over. It was—over—long ago,' she faltered.

'No! It's not. Not as long as you remember—or think you remember—and you were a child, and believed only what you were told. You think I didn't know who you were that night at James' house? You think I didn't know that you'd gone under protest, to please them?' His voice was filled with contempt. 'Answer me, Arwenna. At least do me that courtesy.'

'All right. Yes! I did go "under protest", as you put it. I didn't want to meet you again. I didn't want to have anything to do with you.' She lifted her head. 'Does that answer satisfy you?'

'No, not yet. I want to know exactly what you heard.'

'You must know what you did——'

'No. I said what *you heard*. There's a vast differ-ence between the fact 'and the fantasy. Why do you think I vowed to come back one day? Why do you think I'd vowed to show everyone I wasn't afraid?' He looked at her across the room, across time itself, and he was like a giant, tall and unafraid of anything. She couldn't imagine he ever had known fear.

'You're going to hear the truth at last. You're not going to like it, so you'd better sit down, Arwenna.'

'No, I'll stand.' He began to walk towards her. The time for fear had passed. There was an inevitability now to everything. Arwenna remained standing where she was, and when he was a foot or so away he stopped. They faced each other.

'Very well,' said Garth. 'Like this. So be it.' He took off his jacket and tie and laid them down on a chair. Then he began to undo his shirt. Disbelieving, rooted to the spot, Arwenna could only stand and watch. She didn't believe it, but it was happening. She looked as he took his shirt off, and he was deeply tanned, and muscular, and broad-shouldered. She wanted to look away, but she couldn't. With his eyes upon her, grim and cold, he said : 'Now look at my back,' and as he said it he turned away from her, so that she was staring, transfixed, at the broad back—the back that had a long, ugly, livid scar running diagonally from his left shoul-der to his waist. 'You can see that,' he said, and picked up his shirt again. Turning, he began to put it on. 'But you don't know who gave it to me, do you?'

She shook her head, unable to speak. But in a dread-ful way she sensed what his next words would be, and she wanted to stop them, but there was nothing she could do that would make this happen. Nothing.

CHAPTER SEVEN

'BEFORE I tell you,' said Garth, 'I want you to tell me why you hated me, what you were told, years ago. Don't be afraid. I'm not going to get angry—or more angry than I am. I'll listen without interruption, and then I'll tell you the truth of the matter.'

She decided that it might be better if she sat down, and he followed suit. Then Arwenna looked at him. 'My father said that you were a troublemaker, a liar and a thief, and that Raneley was better off without you and your family. He wasn't the only one—when you were eighteen or nineteen you'd stolen some money from old Farmer Miller's home—and—beaten him up——' She paused. This was horrible. This was something she had buried at the back of her mind as being so awful that it should never be said, and Garth was making her say it, but now, looking at him, it seemed impossible that she was talking of him fifteen years ago. She saw his face, bleak, hard, implacable, and a shiver ran down her spine. She had always accepted what she had been told as a child—had always believed, because the grown-ups believed it, and they were always right. Yet she had just seen his back—— She held her hands tightly clasped together, and was silent.

'And old Farmer Miller was a friend of your father's, wasn't he?' His voice was taut, tense.

'Yes, he'd helped father out occasionally when the shop wasn't doing well.'

Garth nodded.

'Kind old Farmer Miller was a liar—and a hypocrite. The only difference was that he was respected in the village—and he had money. I was from a poor family,

and I was young.' He stood up and paced the room as
if he could no longer remain still. 'I did beat him up,
as you put it, but I never stole from him. And the
reason I beat him, and the reason I got this memento'
—he gestured to his back—'was because I had seen
him beating—with a whip—the poor simple lad who
worked for him on his farm, and I stopped him.' He
came over to her. 'I used to go swimming with my
friends in the pool near his farm, and sneak home that
way, taking the short cut. I was alone that day, it was
Sunday, and as I passed the farmyard I heard the cries
of pain, looked over the wall to see him lashing the lad
—you won't even remember him, I don't suppose—
because he'd obviously just upset a churn of milk. I
leapt over the wall, and he saw me coming. If I hadn't
turned at the right moment I'd have got the whip across
my face.' He paused. 'Farmer Miller was a big strong
man, about fifty then, big, red-faced, beefy. The youth
he was beating was about your size.' He paused, to let
the words sink in. 'That moment is etched clearly on
my brain for all time : the look on the man's face—he
was enjoying what he was doing—and the look of sheer
terror on poor Ned's. I didn't even feel the pain at the
time—not until afterwards. I took the whip from him,
flung it away, and punched him as hard as I could. I
was as tall then as I am now, but thinner, and Miller
was as tough as old boots—but I gave him a thrashing,
while Ned crawled away, then took to his heels.

'I left Miller in his own yard, sprawled in a heap of
manure, and went home. Within an hour the village
bobby arrived. Miller had told him he'd caught me
breaking in, had tried to stop me, and got beaten for his
pains. Who do you think the policeman believed? I was
nineteen, I worked on a building site, I came from a
poor family, and I drove a motorbike that had cost me
all my carefully saved up money—but I was branded as
a troublemaker because I was young, and because I

couldn't prove my story. Ned had gone, run off. Miller's wife—as I found out afterwards, when it was too late—was too terrified of him to do anything else but corroborate his story of the break-in.

'My parents believed me, but that wasn't much help to me. Miller then announced that he wouldn't charge me, and everything was dropped. He was a clever man. Had it come to court they would have had to find Ned, and the real truth would have come out. He was the noble farmer—and I was a young thug, best avoided. My parents became ill with the shame of it—mud sticks, you know—and we moved away. That was when I vowed I'd return one day, with money, and show them. I wanted my revenge on Miller for the unhappiness he'd caused my family—but I never got the chance, because he died of a stroke two years later, when I was just beginning to make money.' He stopped, looked at her. 'There's one person knows the truth—his widow. She still lives at the farm. She's about seventy now. I went to see her a month ago, when I was negotiating for Raneley Hall, and she recognised me. After all those years she recognised me, and I think for a moment that she honestly thought I'd come back for revenge. She's a frail, timid creature, who's lived with the knowledge of her husband's lies all these years. I told her simply that I had no quarrel with her, that I just wanted to let her see that although I was coming back to live in Raneley, I bore her no ill will. Then I left her.'

Arwenna sat, tense and shaking when he had finished. There was the ring of truth to his words that no lies could ever have. There was one question she had to ask however.

'Why, if you had so many bitter memories of Raneley, did you still want to go back there to live?' she asked.

He walked to the window and looked out. 'I'll tell

you that some other time,' he said. Then he turned round to her. 'You're not ready to hear it yet.' He looked at his watch. 'I'm hungry.'

Arwenna stood up. 'I'll go and get some food for us.'

She went into the kitchen, and there she leaned against the sink for a few minutes before moving. There was much more that Garth hadn't told her, some deep instinct within her was sharply aware of that, but he had told her all that he intended to for now. She felt the strangeness of the day's incidents, and they seemed to crowd in on her, and she was as exhausted as if she had run for miles. This deep, complex, fascinating man was like no other. Nothing was ever what it seemed—or was it? She was confused, bewildered, no longer the self-assured person she had been only days ago. Could there be a deeper, subtle reason for his return? Could it be that when he helped Colonel Rhodes, he would take over, cleverly, as he seemed to do in everything else? She stood very still. And after he had taken over —what then? Closure?—people out of work—people from Raneley—the townspeople who had turned their backs on him years before. And she might be helping him to do just that. By her agreeing to work for him, everything would go ahead as planned.

She turned sharply, hearing him come in. Eyes wide, she looked at him. 'What is it now?' he asked, voice hard.

'Colonel Rhodes—you're going to help him?'

'You know I am. That was agreed,' he answered.

'Yes, but I didn't know then about—what you've just told me. Is that what you plan? To close the place? To take over—then to—to——'

'Have my revenge at last?' he laughed. 'There's a thought!'

'Is it?' she demanded.

Garth looked at her, eyes narrowed. 'Is that what you think?'

'I think—anything's possible—with you.'

'Very true. And what do you intend to do about it? That is—of course—if that's what I plan.' And he smiled.

'Tell James' father.'

'And what do you think he could do?' He crossed the floor to her. 'He has no money, it'll close anyway, and he'll be bankrupt in a year if nothing's done.'

'Yes, so you say—but how much cleverer if *you* do it!'

'Is that how your mind works?'

She shivered. 'I don't know. I feel confused. All I wanted was yes or no——'

'Not from me. You intrigue me, Arwenna.' He put his hands on her bare arms. 'You intrigue me very much. Would it matter so terribly to you——'

'Of course it would.' She looked at him, calmer now, her strength and natural resilience helping her to cope with this powerful force of him.

'Yes, I see that it would. You care for Raneley, and its people, don't you?'

'Of course, I do! I can see that, for you, it's different——' She stopped.

'Very,' he said dryly. 'How much do you care?'

'What do you mean?'

'I'll tell you in a moment. First, I'll tell you that I'm planning to buy other businesses in and around Raneley. The large store there—it's for sale, but you wouldn't know that—the row of shops and houses on the main road——'

'Where our café is?'

Garth looked faintly surprised. 'Why, yes, so it is.'

'But it's rented. The landlord is——'

'A company in nearby Chesterfield, Green & Dutton, acting for an elderly gentleman who wants to sell.'

'Oh, my God!' she whispered. 'You're planning a take-over?'

'Not necessarily. And why should that be a bad thing?'

'Because of what I know.'

He released her and turned away, and opened the refrigerator door. 'What do you want to eat?'

'Nothing. I'm not hungry.'

He looked at her. 'Were you before?'

'I was——'

'But not now?'

'No.' She shook her head.

Garth fetched out a carton of eggs. 'I'm sure you could force an omelette down, couldn't you?'

'No, but I'll make you one if you want,' she said dully. There was a heavy weight in her stomach, almost a pain. How could anyone fight a man like this? She took the carton from him and began to search for a pan.

'Thank you. This is all supposition on your part, you know,' he told her, watching her break three eggs into a basin.

'Then your motives are all good?'

He shrugged. 'Are anyone's?'

'It doesn't answer the question.'

'It's not intended to. Perhaps you should work things out for yourself. Think. Think hard—and see what you come up with, Arwenna.'

'You're talking riddles.' She beat vigorously at the egg whites with a fork, and he began:

'There's an electric mixer——'

'I don't need one. I make a better omelette my way,' she answered, and redoubled her efforts. It saved her from screaming. The sheer physical exercise helped her.

'You know what I want,' he said, and she knew his words didn't refer to omelettes, or mixers. She knew, suddenly, what they meant. She poured the mixture into the pan with the heated oil in it, and it bubbled up instantly; she added salt and pepper, and reached over for the spatula. But everything was automatic, she was numbed with the sudden realisation. And he turned her round to face him, and held her there, and said: 'Yes, I can see that you know.' He said it very softly.

'You want me.' Garth nodded. 'No,' she said. '*No*. You've done enough already. I'm working for you. It was to help—James' father—to help him. Yet now it seems I've landed him further in it.'

'But it needn't be that. And I needn't buy those other places——'

'If I sleep with you?' she demanded.

He gave her a crooked smile. 'Would that be too high a price to pay?'

'I wouldn't even consider it,' she said coldly, and, freeing herself, turned away from him.

'You've had lovers. You're not a naïve virgin.'

'You believed that?' Her eyes flashed angrily.

'Wasn't I expected to? The Belgian who proposed in bed——'

'He had 'flu. *He* was in bed, *I* wasn't. We were at his family house, and they were there as well.'

'Ah!' Garth seemed amused. 'And the wealthy Philippe?' He held up his hand. 'Wait—let me guess. You didn't mention his age. He was about ninety-seven?'

'The other end—twelve. I was looking after him with the other children.'

'So I was right,' he drawled.

'Meaning?' she snapped. She turned away, tipped out the cooked omelette on to a plate and banged it down on the table, suddenly angry.

'I knew,' he shrugged. 'No, I *guessed*—that you hadn't—and James? You've never——?' he paused, mouth twitching delicately.

'No, never,' she said flatly. 'Satisfied?' She glared at him, at the darkening eye. 'I wish I'd blacked them both while I was at it!'

She was interrupted by his shout of laughter, and he caught hold of her, and he was shaking. 'Let me go!' she snapped furiously, and stamped hard on his foot. 'Just let me—Mmm——'

Garth kissed her, stopping her words, blotting them out in mid-sentence; he kissed her hard and long, and held her tightly to him, and looked down at her when he had done; his eyes were dark and intense, and his face was not smiling now, not at all. 'I want you,' he said, 'more than I've ever wanted any woman——'

'Only because you can't have me. You're like a child trying to get a toy that's out of reach—you expect me to fall into bed with you just because you're *you*,' she said, breathless after the kiss, and trying hard not to let him see the effect. 'But I've gone as far as I'm going with you, do you understand?'

She tried to push herself free of him. 'Let me go, please.'

'Make me,' he said softly.

'I can hurt you. I know how to hurt a man——'

He released her, and she thought her threat had frightened him, and she managed to smile—just before she was twisted round so that he was behind her, and now holding her, and there was no way that she could fight that. 'Now,' he whispered, 'let's see——'

Arwenna twisted, she tried to turn, she reached up her one free hand and tried to grasp hold of his hair, but he laughed, and evaded her, then caught that hand, and she was totally helpless. Exhausted, she gasped: 'What are you trying to prove? That you're smarter than me?'

'That I can kiss you any time I want,' he said, and eased her slightly round, and then did so. It was strange, being held like that, so helpless and secure, and being kissed, sideways on, as it were, and it was oddly exciting. Her heart began to thud, and she tried to free her lips from his, but only because she knew she should, not because she wanted to.

Garth's mouth left a lingering trail of fire across her cheek, then he kissed her hair, then the back of her neck, which made her shiver all over, so sudden and unexpected was it. Then he said: 'See?'

'Your omelette's getting cold,' she said shakily, and he released her, looked at her, then sat down.

Arwenna remained standing where she was. She wondered if her face was pink. It felt warm, she felt warm all over. 'You're a swine,' she muttered.

'This omelette is good,' he answered. 'Sure you don't want anything?'

'No. I said—you're a swine.'

'I heard you. What do you want me to do? Burst into tears? I've been called worse.'

'That I can believe.' She wanted to hit him, to hurt him, and she didn't know how—or why.

'Will you make me a cup of coffee?' he asked.

'No! Make your own.' She whirled away and then filled the kettle.

'Changed your mind?'

'No. I'm making myself one,' she snapped.

'Leave enough water for me.'

'Go to hell!' She switched on the kettle and fetched a beaker from the cupboard. Garth finished his omelette and took the plate to the sink, then got a beaker for himself. He stood beside her, and when the kettle had boiled, and she had poured the water on to the instant coffee, he followed her. She walked out into the main lounge and went over to the window. There she stood looking out over the buildings, seeing the traffic passing below, the busy hubbub of daily life, everyone going about their business unaware of her watching, not caring anyway, then she looked over to the clinic, imagining her aunt resting, perhaps sleeping now, but recovering. She wished it was all over and she was back in Raneley, with James, living a normal every-

day life, helping her aunt, planning her wedding to
James, looking for somewhere to live, saving up—and
it suddenly seemed wrong. She frowned. James—she
loved James, he loved her. But she hadn't really given
him a thought since yesterday. He seemed very far
away, distant, almost a stranger. She tried to conjure
him up in her mind, and all she saw was the mocking
face of the man she had just told to go to hell.

'James,' she whispered, and a voice from behind her
said:

'Why don't you phone him?' She whirled round,
spilling some coffee. She hadn't heard Garth approach.

'Do you always creep around?' she demanded
angrily.

'I walk quietly. That's not creeping,' he answered
mildly for him. 'I didn't want to interrupt your reverie.'

'Well, you did,' she snapped. 'You nearly made me
spill my coffee.'

'That's your nerves to blame, not my fault.'

'There's nothing wrong with my nerves—or wasn't
before I met you, thank you,' she retorted.

'Really? Is that the effect I have on you? Shame! I'd
hoped for something different.'

'Why don't we get on with some work?' she sighed.
'At least you're fairly normal then.'

'That was the idea, I thought. Work, I mean, not me
being normal. That's something I can't comment on. I
consider myself perfectly normal.'

'You're about as normal as—as—a bulldozer in
a——' Arwenna sought for words—'in a sweetshop,'
she finished.

'Surely you can do better than that?' he commented,
amused, smiling broadly. 'Never mind. Sit down, drink
your coffee, and think about it. Incidentally, I'd better
give you some money. What salary did we agree on?'

'We didn't.' She wished he wouldn't keep switching

the conversation around, as though nothing was wrong.

'Ah, no, we didn't. Will a hundred do you?'

'A hundred a month?'

'A week.'

'A hundred pounds a *week*?' she gasped.

'Not enough? A hundred and ten, then.'

'That's ridiculous! I've never earned that much in my life!'

'Don't look so startled,' he grinned. 'A good secretary can earn that, and more.'

'I'm not a secretary.'

'A translator, then. And you're a good one.'

'You're not joking? You mean it?'

'I'm not joking.'

Arwenna sat down. Now was the time to tell him. 'I'm going to pay you back for Aunt Daisy's operation,' she said. 'I was going to save up as much as I could of what you paid me but I didn't think it would be that amount. I'll be able to repay you sooner than I thought, if you'll tell me how much, roughly——'

'I thought that was already settled,' said Garth. 'I undertook that responsibility. It was part of our agreement.'

'Part of the blackmail, you mean,' she said. 'No. That's *my* responsibility don't you see? She's my aunt. The other—Colonel Rhodes—that's different——'

'Different? They're family too—or going to be—aren't they?'

'*Yes!* But——' She stopped. What's the matter with me? she thought.

'But?' he enquired.

She shook her head. 'It's different, that's all.'

Garth sat down beside her on the settee. 'Let's get to work,' he said. 'I'll give you your money later. You'd prefer cash?'

'If possible.'

'It's possible.' He picked up a sheet of paper she hadn't seen before, and handed it to her. 'Read that, and tell me what you think.'

Work was resumed. Gradually the atmosphere became normal, her jangled nerves were soothed; she concentrated on what they were doing. Garth too was different now. It was like seeing another man in action. Incisive, cool and logical, still forceful, but in a different way. Arwenna could always appreciate a brain such as he possessed. She felt as though she was learning something from him all the time, and when he fetched in balance sheets and a calculator, and asked her how she was on maths, she told him that she was quite a whiz with these too, and he laughed and said he'd thought as much, and gave them to her to do, and the atmosphere was as near pleasant as it could ever be, with them.

When the telephone rang she left him to visit the bathroom, and looked at herself critically in the mirror as she washed her hands. Her face glowed, her eyes were bright and sparkling. She felt more alive than she had ever done in her life. She felt vibrant, alert—she pulled a face at herself and went back to join Garth. He was still talking, but it was about money and didn't seem to concern her, so she went back to the kitchen, made coffee, and feeling very hungry, found a tin of biscuits and ate three.

He hung up as she went in. 'Sorry about that,' he said. 'Ah, coffee! Good.'

He sat down. 'Let's have a break. What are we doing tonight—after visiting Aunt Daisy, I mean?'

'*We?* Don't you have friends to see or anything? I'm quite happy to watch television sometimes—please don't feel——'

'There's a good film on at nine. Okay, that's settled. We'll visit Aunty, call in at a little Indian take-away I know—er—you do like curry, I hope?'

'Yes, but——'

'Bring a curry back here and watch the film.'

He watched her face, apparently puzzled, frowned, and added: 'Don't you want a curry? We can get a Chinese—or eat out, of course.'

'No, it's not that.' But what was it? Arwenna didn't know herself.

'Look,' said Garth, 'I'd like to make a few phone calls, and I was going to go to the office to collect some things. It's nearly four now, I'll phone them and get them dropped off. I think we'll call it a day with this lot for now. Do you want to do any shopping?'

Arwenna was feeling more confused by the minute. It was like standing on quicksands—although she never had—but she was beginning to know what it might feel like. She nodded. It seemed easier to agree with him.

'Good. I'll get your money, phone for a taxi. It'll take you and bring you back. Where do you want to go? Oxford Street—Piccadilly——?'

'I don't know.' She looked up at him as he went towards the telephone.

'Better decide. Why not call at Harrods, buy some clothes? I've got an account there.' He turned round and regarded her gravely. 'Buy something to wear tomorrow night.'

'Tomorrow night?' she queried.

'We're going out, remember? Bill Chisholm?' he explained.

'Oh, yes, of course.' She had forgotten.

'Get yourself a nice dress. Please,' he added.

'I can't afford it——'

'On my account.'

'Oh, No!' She stood up and went over to him. 'No, I'd rather not. I don't have to explain why, do I?'

'It's not buying you, if that's what you mean. Call it a bonus, a perk, for working so hard.' He smiled. 'And you do. Besides, you'll need clothes for France.'

'You don't understand,' she said fiercely. 'You said you can't let anyone take you over, but you're doing it now. Clothes—what next? It's not—it's not——'

'Right? Of course it damned well is. You've got to dress the part if you're working for me. We'll be travelling incognito, don't forget, next week, as ordinary tourists, not prospective buyers. I want to see how those hotels are run, without them knowing who I am. Now, I insist you buy some clothes, anything you like —you've got good taste—and we'll talk about payment later, when we return.'

'And do you think James will appreciate your reasoning?' she asked.

'He doesn't have to know.'

'He's not stupid. He knows what I can and can't afford.'

'The last time you spoke to him he accused you of sleeping with me. Why haven't you rung him to get that little matter sorted out?'

'I——' she began, and stopped.

'Why?' he asked.

'I don't know,' she whispered. She looked at the silent telephone. It seemed very accusing.

'Phone him now. From your room, if you like.'

'He'll be at work.'

'Phone him there.'

'We were talking about clothes a moment ago——' she began feebly.

'So we were. Well, are you going to call him—or shall I?'

'No.' She shook her head.

'I have to phone his father,' added Garth. 'That's one of the calls I must make when you go out. There's nothing wrong with me talking to him as well, is there?'

'Yes, there is. I don't want you to.'

'Very well. But you should.'

'Why are you so concerned all of a sudden?' demanded Arwenna. 'You don't give a damn about him.'

'I wonder if *you* do,' he said, and the words hung in the air, and she turned away because she didn't want him to look into her eyes and know the truth, and he said softly : 'Look at me, Arwenna.'

'No,' she said. 'No——' But she knew what he was doing, even with her back turned, sensed his movement behind her, then his hands, drawing her round to face him, and she stood helpless before him, unable to look away again.

Garth didn't speak. He looked deep into her eyes for an endless, shimmering moment, and then slowly, reluctantly, it seemed, he released her.

'Phone him,' he said at last. 'Tell him you don't love him.'

Her mouth trembled. 'How do you know?'

'I know.'

'You're wrong——'

'I'm not wrong. I know. You don't love him now, you probably never have. Isn't it kinder to tell him?'

'We're engaged to be married——'

'Engagements can be broken off. That's the whole point of them. A testing time, a period of waiting before total commitment.'

'It will hurt him——' she began.

'Not as much as if you waited until after you were married——'

'It's what you want, isn't it? For us to finish?'

'Yes, it is.'

'So that *you* can have me? Is that it? Do you think I'm going to fall into your arms once he's safely out of the way?'

'There's certainly more of a chance of it.'

'There's no chance,' she said, voice husky with emotion. 'Not with a man like you—not for me—don't you see? You'd take over my life, tell me what to think, to eat, to wear—you're doing it now, and, God knows, we don't even love each other!'

'But we are attracted to each other.'

'Perhaps. I don't know. But you said it yourself. We're two of a kind—The irresistible force meeting the immovable object, then—bang! Nothing. No, thanks. Not me. Not me—ever.' She was shaking, her voice was husky, quiet, so that he had to move near her to hear. His face was grim, and his voice, when he answered her, was harsh.

'There's no way I can change,' he said. 'Not for you —not for anybody. I am as I am.'

'You're powerful, you're almost overwhelming, you could be dangerous—I know that, I saw that the first moment I met you at James' house—yes, I admit it, I was as aware of something—I don't know what, the minute we looked at each other across that room. I still don't know what it is. I only know you've turned my life over, perhaps made me see some things more clearly—you've forced me to work for you, and I'm doing so, and I'll work hard, for the time we have together—but then, when it's over, when the year has passed, that's it. You may still live in Raneley, I don't know. I don't know how long you intend to stay—I don't know much about you at all, and I'm not sure if I want to. I've never met anyone like you before, and I may not again, but we have no real part in each other's lives, because we would eventually destroy one another.' She finished, and she was shaking like a leaf, and only her determination had carried her this far. 'Don't you *see*?'

'Oh yes, I see,' Garth said softly. 'And of course you're right. We both know the truth of what you say. There's only one thing you seem to have forgotten.'

'And what's that?' she whispered.

'We've neither of us ever loved. You've never loved James, nor, I suspect, any other man. Am I right?'

Arwenna nodded slowly. 'And I've never loved any woman. I've made love, I've had affairs, yes, that—but I've never fallen in love with any woman. Perhaps, then, neither of us is capable of it. Doesn't that worry you?'

'No. Does it worry you?'

'No.' They looked at each other across an unbridgeable gulf, and the physical attraction was an almost tangible force, touching them both. It was Arwenna who looked away first. The tension was unbearable. 'So it might be better for us to work it out of our systems,' he said. 'Then we'll be free.'

'Have an affair? That's what you mean, isn't it?'

'What else do you think I mean?' he asked, and took her in his arms and held her to him.

CHAPTER EIGHT

SHE wanted him—that was the awful thing. She wanted him to make love to her. She gently disengaged herself from his arms and looked at him, seeing him more clearly than she had ever seen any other man. Now was the time for her to be strong. Now, not later, when it would be too late to see clearly any more.

'Thanks, but no, thanks!' she said. 'I find your offer almost irresistible. You certainly have a charming— and direct—way of expressing your desires. Work it out of our systems, indeed! You talk as if we have a dose of 'flu——' She turned away. 'Will you please call me a taxi, I'll go and leave you to your phone calls, and then we'll talk about this evening.'

She walked steadily away from him, and heard him pick up the telephone as she went out of the room. She combed her hair vigorously, looking at her face in the

mirror, wondering if it betrayed her to him. If he knew
—if he ever guessed, she would be lost. If Garth even
had the faintest idea that she wanted him to make love
to her she would have no chance of getting away. That
consideration was so strong that it was several minutes
before she remembered the other shattering realisation that had come to her. She had known, in an instant
of time, when he had said those fatal words: 'I wonder
if *you* do.' She had seen everything so vividly that it
was as if her life for the past year had flashed in front
of her. No, she didn't love James. She never had, not
truly. She had imagined herself to be in love with him,
and that was a world away from what she knew now.

He would be hurt. That was one reason why she
would not ring him at work. He would be angry as
well, but how angry she was not, fortunately, at that
moment able to imagine. She sighed, put down her
comb, and went back into the main lounge. Into her
bag she had put her banker's card. If she bought a
dress, it would be with her own money, not Garth's.
The only money she would take from him would be
for work.

He was waiting, and he had an envelope which he
handed to her. 'Don't get mugged,' he told her.

'I'll try not to. Thank you.' She put the envelope
into her handbag. 'Shall I go down?'

'The taxi's on its way. I'll be here when you get
back.' Garth went to open the door, and the lift was
waiting, and he watched her into it. 'Think about what
I said,' He looked at her very directly as he spoke, and
he wasn't smiling any more.

'I already have.' Arwenna closed the lift doors and
pressed the button, and twenty minutes later she was
wandering round Harrod's, and had managed to put
both James and Garth from her mind.

She didn't, after all, have a lot of time to shop there,
didn't see anything she fancied—or not at the price she

could afford—and was on her way out when a voice hailed her, an unmistakable loud, cheerful voice, 'Hey, Arwenna!'

She turned, on the pavement, nearly caused a minor traffic jam as the hurrying crowds swerved to avoid her, and saw a tall lanky bearded figure loping towards her from the roadway. He was waving and grinning all over the little of his face she could see, and he scooped her up in his arms and hugged her delightedly.

'It *is* you! I thought I was dreaming! What the heck are you doing in London? Why didn't you phone?' he asked, and Arwenna, laughing, said:

'Put me down and I'll tell you.' She looked into the blue eyes of Steven Marshall, the student she had met in Paris a couple of years previously—the one with whom she would have got in touch if accommodation had been difficult. He looked delighted to see her, and kept hold of her arm as if she might run away if he let go. 'I'm staying here for a few days while my aunt has an operation,' she answered. 'It's good to see you, Steve. I was going to phone you. Are you still at the same place?'

'Yes, four of us now, in a grotty flat. I'm just on my way back there now.' He gestured towards a crammed plastic carrier bag he had put on the ground, much to the danger of passers-by, and scooped it up. 'My turn to do the shopping.' A long French loaf peeped out, and the bag seemed otherwise to be full of vegetables. 'Come on, let's have a coffee somewhere.'

'I haven't got time——' Arwenna began weakly, and he took her arm firmly and began steering her along the crowded pavement.

'Yes, you have. I want to hear what you've been doing.' He opened the glass doors of a small café and found a table, then loped off towards the counter, leaving Arwenna with his shopping bag.

'Right,' he said, and sat opposite her, after deposit-

ing two cups of espresso coffee on the plastic-topped
table. 'My treat, you notice.'

'Thank you. The last of the big spenders,' she
grinned, and he raised his fist in mock threat.

'Watch it, half pint, I'm bigger than you,' he
answered.

'You're bigger than everybody,' she conceded. 'Look,
we've exchanged insults now, so how are you, and
what are you doing? And how's Zack?'

'I'm fine—I'm taking a post-graduate course in eco-
nomics—and Zack is still pining for you. Any more
questions?' He took hold of her left hand and grimaced.
'Hmm, still engaged. Zack won't like that.'

Arwenna took her hand away. 'Actually, I'm
not——' She had forgotten the ring.

'Then why are you wearing it?'

She sighed. 'I—I only decided this afternoon.' She
looked at him. He was a whole world away from Garth,
he and Zack, in age, temperament, background—he
was refreshing to see. She was glad she had bumped
into him, for it would have been so easy to forget to
telephone him.

'Well, that calls for celebration—or does it?' He
looked at her shrewdly. He was easily as intelligent as
Garth. She had known him and Zack for only a matter
of weeks, when they had been in Paris, but she had
spent a lot of her free time with them, and had estab-
lished an easy-going relationship that would endure, as
some friendships did, for ever. She liked them both
equally, and knew they were fond of her, and though
their letters had been spasmodic, there had never been
a shortage of things to say. James had never understood the friendship, so she rarely mentioned them to
him. Now it wouldn't matter anyway ...

'Neither. I'd rather not talk about it, Steve,' she
answered gently.

'Fair enough. What are you doing tonight? We're

having some friends round for a spaghetti supper—you know what a whizz I am at the old spaghetti Bolognese——' he kissed his fingers, eyes closed in ecstasy, and she laughed.

'I'd love to, but I've got to see my aunt.'

'After then? I'll pick you up. Where are you staying?'

She looked at him. That was too long a story to tell. But why not go? Why *not*?

'All right,' she answered. 'What do you mean, you'll pick me up?' Her eyes gleamed with mischief.

'I have a *car*, my dear girl,' he said proudly. 'I *did* tell you, in one of my many *long* letters which I don't suppose you bothered to read——'

'I did, I did,' she protested. 'I'd forgotten, that's all. Anyway, you shouldn't be able to afford a car.'

'Daddy's softened up in his old age,' he answered. 'Gave me a Mini for my last birthday, but I'm not mad enough to drive it into town. Okay, give me your address.' He whipped out an envelope and stub of pencil from the pocket of the faded and well patched denim jacket he wore, and held the pencil poised expectantly.

Arwenna sighed. 'Look, Steve, can I make a phone call first? I'm staying at a man's flat'—he raised his eyebrows, but said nothing—'and if I phone him and tell him first I think it would be better.'

'A man? You naughty thing! And here was I thinking you'd kept yourself pure for me all these years——' Steve gave a disappointed sigh.

'Believe me, it's platonic, *and* it's a long story, which I'll tell you later. Okay?' She stood up. There was a pay telephone at the rear of the café. 'Got a five?'

He handed her one. 'Don't be long, we've got a lot of news to catch up on.'

'I won't.'

The first time she rang the line was engaged. She put

the phone down and waited, looked back to see Steve
sitting sipping his coffee and watching her. She dialled
again and it was answered immediately.

'Vanner.' The familiar voice sounded almost staccato
over the line.

'Garth? It's me, Arwenna. I've met an old friend
who's asked me round this evening, so I said I'd phone
you first to check if it was all right. He'll pick me up
in his car——'

'Where does he live?' he cut in.

She frowned, trying to remember. 'Oh, Hampstead way—why?'

'I'll take you. You're coming back here first to visit
your aunt, aren't you?'

'Yes, of course. I'm on my way now.'

'Where are you?'

'In a café near Harrod's.'

'Have you ordered a taxi yet?'

'No. I was going to get one when I bumped into
Steve.'

'I'll pick you up there if you like in about half an
hour. I have to go out—what's the name of the place?'

'I haven't a clue.' She felt faintly annoyed. 'Look, I
can get myself home quite easily——'

'Just tell me the name of the café. You'll not get a
taxi at this time of day.' Garth sounded impatient.
Arwenna turned and looked at the counter. Over it
was the name, which she told him. 'I'll see you outside.
Half an hour from now. Goodbye.'

'Good——' The line went dead. Arwenna hung up
and walked back to Steve and sat down.

'Wow!' he exclaimed. 'Had a row? You look good
and mad.'

'Do I?' She simmered down immediately. 'Sorry. He
says he'll bring me to your place. And he's picking me
up from here in half an hour.' She sighed. 'He's a very
busy man.'

'Hmm, sounds it. Who is he? Or is that none of my business?'

'Of course it is. You won't know him. His name's Garth Vanner, and I'm working for him, and he's paid for my aunt to have an operation at his friend's clinic, and as he lives literally only a short walk away from the clinic, I'm staying there at his place.'

'That's put it in a nutshell. Vanner? I've heard of him—who hasn't? He's a real whizz kid, isn't he? Property millionaire?'

'That's the one.'

'How on earth did you get to work for him? I mean, living in a godforsaken little place like Raneley——'

'How dare you!' She slapped his hand. 'It's a lovely town!'

'Sorry, course it is, my sweet, but you know what I mean. It's hardly the hub of the universe.'

'He comes from there, and he's just bought a house there,' she explained. 'That's how I came to meet him, through James——'

'With whom,' Steve cut in, 'you have just severed relations.' He leered amiably at her. '*Vairy* interesting,' he drawled, in a heavy foreign accent.

You don't know the half of it, she thought wryly, and smiled at him. 'Oh, Steve, I'm so glad to see you, honestly. You're like a breath of fresh air.'

'Is this Vanner revolting or something?' he asked.

'No, he's not. He's a very attractive man—hard, ruthless, but very attractive——'

'And lusting after you?' he asked, too shrewdly by far.

'What makes you say that?' But her telltale colour gave her away.

'Come on, ducky, it's obvious, isn't it? You're a damned attractive wench, and *I've* been lusting quietly after you for two years or so, and so's Zack, and any other red-blooded male you set eyes on.'

Arwenna grinned impishly. 'You do me good!'

'I love you, Arwenna, you know that. I wouldn't want to see you hurt, ever.' Steve's eyes told the truth of his words, and he took both her hands and held them, oblivious to people sitting at the other tables. 'I don't love you in a possessive way, but in that special way that good friends will always have—and I want you to be happy.' He gave a rueful grin. 'Hell, I never thought I'd sit in a café with you making this kind of speech, but I care for you very deeply, and I always will, whatever other relationships we might have.' His face went serious. 'If anyone ever hurt you badly, I think I would want to kill them.'

'Oh, Steve!' His words had a curious effect on her. He was normally so lighthearted, walking through the world with an easy grace and charm, living life fully, one of nature's genuinely well balanced people who attract others like magnets, that his words were all the more moving. 'I love you too, in a special kind of way. And don't worry, no one's going to hurt me. I'm quite tough, remember?'

He grinned. 'You're all woman, too. Have we time for another coffee? I need one after that speech.'

'Why not? My treat.' Arwenna picked up her bag and went to the counter. They had another twenty minutes or so, no more. Garth wouldn't be able to park outside. She took the coffees back to the table, then asked Steve to tell her about his flat. He wrote down the directions how to get there, and she heard all about the other two flatmates, and the time passed swiftly and easily.

Then it was time to go. As they went outside Steve took her hand and kissed it. 'See you later, Arwenna. About eight—eight-thirty?'

'Yes, I'm looking forward to it. Off you go. Give Zack my love.'

'I will. He might even shave for you, who knows? Miracles have happened before.'

He stooped to kiss her cheek as a sleek Daimler purred to a halt at the curb. Arwenna saw it out of the corner of her eye and quickly turned her face and kissed Steve. 'He's here,' she whispered. 'Goodbye.'

She ran towards the car, and Steve watched her go with a strange expression on his face, a very sad expression that vanished as he waved to her, then turned away.

Garth drove on. For a few minutes the traffic occupied him fully, then, when they had turned into a comparatively quiet street, he asked: 'Was that your friend?'

'Yes.'

'And you have his address?'

'Yes. In my bag, with directions.'

'That's good.' Nothing more was said. Garth didn't seem annoyed at having to meet her. He didn't seem curious about Steve. He seemed just like a stranger. They drove straight back to his flat, and when they were in he commented: 'I see you didn't buy any clothes.'

'No. I didn't see anything I wanted.' Arwenna flung her bag down on a chair. 'I'd like to have a shower now if I may.'

'Of course you may. After we've visited your aunt I'll take you to your friend's flat. Give me the address and I'll check if I know where it is.'

She handed him the envelope in silence. He *was* like a stranger. She felt as if she couldn't talk to him at all. It was as though some shutters had gone down. He was remote, polite, and his face was expressionless. He read the address and the directions, in Steve's careless scrawl, then looked up. 'I'll find it,' he said.

'I'd like to phone James before we go.'

'If you must.' His eyes, as he looked at her, were like stone. 'I've made all my calls. What time are you planning staying on until?'

'I don't know. About eleven——' Damn the man! Did he think he could make her feel guilty at wanting to go out? 'I can make my own way back here, so please don't worry about that.'

'On your own? At night? Don't be stupid, Arwenna,' he said dismissively. 'You're not in Raneley now——'

'Not on my own,' she interrupted. 'I'd get lost anyway. Steve's got a car.'

'Oh, has he? And will he have been drinking?'

'He's not a teetotaller, if that's what you mean. Yes, probably.'

'Then I'll pick you up.'

'And aren't *you* going to have a drink all evening? How *noble*,' she said sarcastically.

'Probably not. And if I were to, I'd come in a taxi. I'm not stupid.'

'Oh, no, you're not. You're just bloody perfect, that's all,' she snapped. 'And I am over twenty-one, you know, and not entirely helpless. I'm quite capable of phoning for a taxi for myself, you know, if necessary, so don't think you have to be nursemaid!'

'I'm responsible for you being here. And while you are here I'll see that you don't get lost, or have to wander the streets at night. That's common courtesy, not "nursemaiding",' he retorted. 'And as I'm not doing anything particular this evening it's no trouble to take you and bring you back.' Said logically and sensibly as his words were, they made Arwenna feel as though she were childish. This was the man who had held her in his arms and told her he wanted to make love to her. It was quite hard for her to believe. He had never loved any woman, he had told her. She could easily believe that. He probably didn't know what love was, and never would.

'Then thank you,' she answered, 'I accept.' She left him standing there and went to her bedroom, closing the door firmly after her. Time to telephone James. It was something that had to be done, and the sooner the better. There was a heavy sick feeling inside her as she picked up the receiver and began to dial. Surely it would be better telling him in person? She hesitated, misdialled, and put the receiver down. Perhaps—now she would prepare him, tell him she would see him when she returned—she picked up the phone again, slightly easier in her mind. She owed him that, at least. The telephone at the other end began to ring.

Arwenna stood by the window of her room and looked out at the gardens, but she saw nothing of them. Her eyes were blurred with tears. Twenty minutes had passed since the call to James, but she stood there oblivious of time.

He had known that something was wrong as soon as she spoke. He had also been waiting for her to telephone since his accusations, and her hanging up on him, and clearly during that time his jealous anger had been silently growing. It had been far more difficult than she had envisaged—and it had ended with him saying, in shaking, bitter tones: 'I don't want to see you when you get back to Raneley—there's nothing to say, is there? We both know we're through—Let's leave it at that. My God, I've been wasting my time, haven't I? You're welcome to him, and he's welcome to *you!*' and he had slammed the receiver down.

Arwenna had tried to call him back, but got the engaged signal. Now she wasn't trying any longer. He had made his opinions clear—that he thought she was having an affair with Garth. He would never have believed the truth. There had not only been anger in his voice, but spite in his words. That had upset her more than anything else, yet in a strange way it had helped

her to realise that there could have been no future
for them together.

She was cold, deathly cold, and she didn't want to
go to Steve's flat. She didn't even feel like facing her
aunt. She put her hand to her aching throat, raw with
unshed tears, and prayed for strength. She didn't hear
the knock at the door, and only turned when it opened
and she heard Garth's voice: 'Are you ready?'

She blinked hard a few times and he came across to
the window. 'James?' he said. Arwenna nodded, unable
to speak. 'I see. You've—told him?'

She didn't answer; she didn't need to. She wanted
someone to hold her, and comfort her, but not him.
Not him.

She cleared her throat. 'I'll be all right in a minute,'
she croaked.

'No, you won't. Not to visit your aunt, you won't.'

She brushed her cheek. 'I *will*. Leave me for a
minute. I'll wash my face——'

'You're coming to have a good stiff drink first, then
we'll get you looking human. For God's sake why didn't
you ring him after?'

'I didn't know it would be that bad,' she retorted,
regaining some of her spirit. If anything would cure
her, it wouldn't be Garth. She'd get no sympathy from
that piece of granite. 'And a drink doesn't solve anything—not for me. It might for *you*.'

'That's it,' he mocked. 'You're doing fine—getting
some of the fire back, instead of standing there looking
as though you'd been kicked.'

'Why don't you leave me alone? I don't need *you*,'
she snapped.

'Leave you to wallow in self-pity? We don't have
time for that. You're going out after, remember? Or
had you forgotten?'

'No. Thank God I am,' she said fervently. 'I'll be
with human beings.'

'And I'm not. Thanks!' His voice was caustic.

'No, you're not,' she answered. She could see him clearly now, not blurred. 'But don't let it worry you. I'm sure it never has. You've probably got a cash register where your heart should be.'

'Then I must need somebody to teach me how to be human, mustn't I?' he grated, not seeming angry at all, although he ought to have been. He suddenly took hold of her hand and held it to his breast. 'What do you feel? Don't you feel anything beating there?'

Arwenna tried to pull her hand away, and instead Garth pulled her nearer to him. 'Well?' he demanded. 'I'm waiting for an answer.'

He had her hand over his heart, and the beat was strong and steady. 'Let me go,' she whispered.

'No.'

'Yes! Let me—go!' She made a superhuman effort to be free, and he began laughing softly.

'You're doing fine,' he said. 'Keep fighting!'

She kicked his leg and twisted herself sideways, but he caught hold of her hair and pulled her to face him, and kissed her very soundly.

'*That's* for kicking me,' he told her, when he had done. 'Got any more little tricks?'

His eyes gleamed darkly. No longer the cool stranger, but a strong man holding her, taunting her, maddening her—holding her very tightly, but not brutally, and knowing his strength, and using it to keep her where he chose, until he was ready to let her go. Knowing the futility of trying to escape, Arwenna stopped struggling, but her eyes blazed defiance.

'I wouldn't waste them on you,' she breathed.

'Pity. I enjoy a good fight, now and again, as long as it doesn't get too rough—and you wouldn't, would you?' He smiled. 'You know what would happen if you did.'

'You're not a man, you're a brute!'

'Well, at least that's one step up from a walking cash register,' he mocked. 'Keep going.'

'Go to hell!'

He let her go, turned away, looked back from the doorway, gave a curious half smile. 'If I do, I won't go alone,' he said. 'Rinse your face and comb your hair and we'll go.'

Arwenna watched the door close after him and clenched her fists. Then she went to wash her face. The strange thing was—and she didn't realise why until much later—that she felt much better. The shattering numbness that had taken her after her call to James had completely gone. She felt alive again. She felt cured.

Five minutes later they were on their way by car to visit Aunt Daisy. She lay in bed, still sleeping, but with more colour in her cheeks than that morning. At Arwenna's kiss she opened her eyes and said sleepily:

'Mmm——' Her voice trailed away. Arwenna sat at the bedside and held the old lady's hand. There was silence for a few moments, then Aunt Daisy said, 'Where's Garth?'

He walked over to her. 'I'm here,' he said, taking her hand.

'That's nice.' Her voice was slurred, and she tried to give him a smile, but it was an effort. 'Black eye?' she said, as if faintly surprised—no more than that.

He laughed. 'I walked into a door.'

'Oh dear.' She had closed her eyes again, as if the effort of speaking had tired her. 'Put on a grated apple poultice—or potatoes—don't forget——' She stopped, and they both realised that she was asleep. The visit passed in no time at all.

Garth was driving Arwenna towards Hampstead then, and remarked dryly: 'I must make a note of those cures for black eyes, they'll probably come in useful. I found your aunt's comment about your mild temper most interesting. I thought she knew you well?'

'She does,' she answered shortly.

'Ah. Meaning that it's I who bring out the worst in you?'

'Got it in one.'

'How strange. Perhaps not, though,' and he smiled slightly, as if something funny had occurred to him.

'What does *that* cryptic remark mean?'

He glanced briefly at her. 'What do you think it means?'

'I don't know. I'm not a mind-reader.'

'Then think. You accused me of being violent, beneath the surface. I told you we were two of a kind—perhaps we are. Perhaps it's all simmering inside with you and you keep it well in check with others.'

'I've never heard anything so ridiculous in my life!' she retorted.

'It's not ridiculous, Arwenna, it's the truth, and you don't like it.'

'Just because you say something it doesn't make it gospel, you know.'

'Perhaps not. But I know you already better than James ever did. That's a fact.'

'You're wrong——' she began, but the words died in her throat. No, Garth wasn't wrong. What he said was true. She closed her eyes briefly, and felt the car slow to turn a corner, and when she opened them again she looked at him.

'Yes,' he said softly. 'And you know it. We're nearly there, Arwenna. Better start looking for the number.'

She gazed out of the window at the endless-seeming row of large old terraced houses on either side of the street. Cars were parked on both sides, and most of the houses were shabby and in need of paint, with scraggy front gardens. She pointed. 'There it is.' The front door was open, and as Garth opened her door, they could hear music drifting down from a wide open attic window. Steve appeared, leaning out, waving. 'Hi! Come on up, both of you.'

Arwenna hoped Garth hadn't heard, but he had. 'Tell him thanks,' he said softly. Steve's head had vanished, to be replaced by Zack's, who nearly fell out of the window as he waved, and Garth turned away towards his car. Arwenna waved back and blew a kiss, and as Garth was about to walk round to his driver's door Steve appeared, ran down the steps, and whirled Arwenna round, hugging her so tightly that she was breathless. Then he looked at Garth and grinned broadly. 'Thanks for bringing her,' he said, and stuck out his hand. 'Steve Marshall.' Garth shook hands with him, and Steve said: 'Would you like to come up for a drink? You're most welcome, honestly.' Garth looked at Arwenna, still within Steve's embrace, then he too smiled—a brief polite one, but a smile, nevertheless.

'Thank you, I will,' he answered, and began to lock the car.

CHAPTER NINE

ALL the furniture in the huge attic room had been pushed back against the poster-filled walls, leaving a large clear area in the centre. A table was filled with cans of beer and bottles, a record player was on full blast in one corner, and the room had about a dozen people in, standing or sitting, talking and drinking. A young bearded man sat crosslegged on a bed, strumming a guitar in silent competition to the music, and seemingly oblivious of it. Steve switched the record player off and clapped his hands loudly, as Zack, as tall as Steve and even more heavily bearded, hugged Arwenna delightedly, declaring his undying love in tones that became very clear as the music stopped.

'Right, everyone,' said Steve. 'Cut that out, Zack, we've got other company. This is Arwenna, and Garth. Arwenna is our one true love, Zack's and mine, so it's hands off, everybody else, and what are you having to drink, Garth? Beer, or cheap disgusting red plonk?'

A roar went up from the others, and a man's voice said: 'It's not plonk. It's best supermarket *vino*, man——' and Arwenna found herself greeting, and being greeted by, the rest of the party. There were only three other girls there, students from the look of them, long-haired, pretty, two in jeans, one in a long flowing flowered skirt and blouse. The guitarist, now able to be heard, struck up a pleasant ballad, and the atmosphere in the room was one of complete accord and harmony.

Garth and Steve stood talking, Garth with glass in hand filled with something that looked like diluted Ribena, while Steve opened a can of beer, and Zack pulled Arwenna away from them into a kitchen overflowing with food and opened tins, and said: 'Let me look at you. God, it's good to see you again!' He grinned down at her. Zack, half American, with dark flashing eyes, and olive skin, who looked more Spanish than anything else. He gave a long sigh. 'It's *good* to see you, honey, really *good*. Even if you had to bring a man with you.' He glanced through the open doorway to where Garth and Steve stood. Both were of the same height, and both, incredibly to Arwenna, seemed to be getting on well. 'You're working for *him*?'

'Yes, Zack, you're looking absolutely splendid. How long has it been? Two years? I can't believe it.'

'Yes, well, I always was a handsome devil. And improving with age.' He forgot about Garth as he gazed fondly at her. 'You too—improving, I mean. You look quite edible. Quite, quite *delicious*.' He bent and kissed her. 'Mmm, taste nice, too. Is *he* staying?'

'I doubt it. Steve asked him up for a drink.'

'I'll get him for that afterwards. I may kill him for it. Here's me, been waiting for this moment for two years, and we're surrounded by people. It's not fair,' he groaned. 'How long are you in London?'

'Only about a week.'

'Hell! Never mind. We'll go out when we can. Does thingy—*him*—let you out alone, or does he have to trail along everywhere?'

'Of course not.' She laughed. 'I'd love to see you, Zack—both of you—any time.'

'Okay, it's a date.' He was about to hug her again when Steve pushed his way in.

'Break it up, you two,' he said. 'Come and join the party. Someone's thundering up the stairs now.' He lowered his voice. 'He's not all that bad, Arwenna— quite human.' Arwenna looked past Steve. Garth was talking to—or rather, being talked to, by two of the girls, who clearly found him an interesting animal in his sober grey suit. He was laughing at something one had said, and the next moment she was refilling his glass. He didn't seem to be protesting.

Two couples burst into the room, and voices were raised in greeting. ''Scuse me,' said Zack. 'Got to go and say hi to this lot. I'll be back.' He slid past Steve and left them.

'Is Garth stopping?' Arwenna asked.

'I dunno. Liz and Jo seem to have nabbed him for themselves. Come on, let's go and get the music going and have a dance. He's a big boy, Arwenna, I'm sure he can take care of himself.'

'You wanted to have a good look at him, didn't you?' she accused.

'Of course!' He grinned down at her. 'Did you give him the black eye?'

She looked at him, her face telling him without

words, and he gave a low whistle. 'You did, you little minx! What had he done? No, don't tell me, I'd rather not know.' He took her round the waist. 'Come on, I'll get you sloshed first, then dance.' Someone had started up the record player, and the new arrivals were doing a fair imitation of disco dancing, urged on by whistles and claps, and the outer door opened again, and the room was suddenly full.

Arwenna found a glass in her hand, and the liquid that looked suspiciously like Ribena was not unpleasant, rather sweet, but clearly harmless. She danced with Steve, then Zack had joined in, and she looked to see Garth having his glass taken from him by Liz—or was it Jo?—and he seemed to be protesting, but laughing as he did so.

The room was very warm. The guitarist had abandoned his efforts to compete with the Bee Gees, and was doing a take-off of John Travolta in a corner, oblivious to the catcalls of his friends. There must have been twenty or more there now, and the noise was unimaginable, and more seemed to be pouring in every moment. A few friends, Steve had said. Arwenna, laughing, realised that she was enjoying herself immensely. She wondered if Garth was, or even if he were still there, because she couldn't see him. As she whirled past the kitchen doorway—she saw. He wasn't alone. Liz—or Jo; Arwenna never had found out who was whom—had her arms round his neck, was standing on tiptoe, and kissing him. He didn't seem in any hurry to escape. And at that precise moment, as she halted with shock, he lifted his face from the fervent embrace and looked directly at her. Arwenna turned away. Garth had taken his jacket off, and his sleeves were rolled up, and his tie was undone.

Steve too had seen. He whirled her away into a dim corner and said: 'He's not doing too badly with

Liz, is he? Better watch it, he may not get out of there alive. Liz is quite a girl.' He laughed. 'Anyway, I can have you to myself now.'

Arwenna didn't know why she was furious, or why the party should suddenly have changed. She glared at Steve, who looked wounded and said quietly : 'Hey, what's the matter?'

'He's disgusting!' she said fiercely.

'You're kidding!' Steve's face was stunned. He put his arms round her, soothing her, holding her tightly. 'It's only a party. I thought he'd be a stuffy bastard—okay, I admit it, I asked him up because I wanted to see his reaction to our little crowd. I've never met a bloated capitalist before—I thought it'd be fun—but he's the one having the fun.' He chuckled, his eyes alight with pleasure. 'He's not bad, honestly.'

Arwenna felt her temper subside. Steve would see good in anybody. And how could she tell him the truth anyway? Garth was even cleverer than she had imagined. He would know what Steve had done, and why. He could have easily refused the invitation. No one would have expected him to fit in with a crowd of students, all in their early twenties, yet that seemed to be precisely what he had done. 'Sorry, Steve,' she said, and smiled at him. 'Can I have another drink?'

'Sure, anything for you.' He kissed the tip of her nose. 'Stay right there. I'll be back.' He returned with two glasses filled with wine, they found a corner of a bed to sit on, and then began to catch up on mutual news. Arwenna put Garth out of her mind.

It was midnight when they left, and the party was beginning to break up. Garth gave four people a lift home, and after he had dropped them off and he and Arwenna were alone in the car, he said :

'That was a very pleasant evening.'

'There's no need to sound surprised when you say

it,' she answered. 'Anyway, I didn't think you'd stay. I wouldn't have thought a students' party was *quite* your scene.'

He laughed. To her sensitive ears, the laughter seemed to hold mockery. 'Oh, I don't know,' he mused. 'It was *very* interesting.'

'So I noticed. I didn't know you went in for girls of twenty,' she said, trying to control her sudden fury.

'Is that what's bothering you? She was a nice girl.'

'It doesn't bother *me*,' she snapped. 'Not one bit. If you want to make a fool of yourself——'

'You weren't doing so badly,' he remarked, with irony. 'Two devoted swains anticipating your every wish—come on, Arwenna, you loved every minute of it.'

'They're old friends,' she retorted, seething.

'Oh, I know. I had Steve telling me all about it. I got the impression that anyone who hurt you would probably get a knife in his back—he thinks the sun shines out of you. As your Aunt Daisy does. Mild-tempered indeed! God, they've not seen the temper in you—and before you cut in, look at you *now*. You're fuming. And why? Because I didn't stand there being stuffy and patronising and looking as though I'd a bad smell under my nose. That's what you'd have liked, isn't it? For me to fall flat on my face—well, I didn't. I know how to get on with anyone I choose, when I choose, and if I happen to want to go and kiss a nubile young woman in a kitchen, or anywhere else for that matter, I won't have *you* telling me what I should be doing instead.' And he switched on the car radio, effectively silencing anything she might have been about to say.

The rest of the journey was accomplished to the sounds of classical music, the kind Arwenna loved, but which had no power to soothe her now. When they reached Garth's flat, she said: 'Thank you for taking me, goodnight,' and stalked off to bed, a bundle of quivering fury. She slammed and locked her bedroom door, not sure if he had been laughing or not, and not wanting to know.

She slept until nearly midday, and was only wakened by the telephone shrilling loudly by her bedside. Fumbling for the receiver, she managed to pick it up, and said, very sleepily: 'Hello?'

'You *are* available? Good.' Garth's voice dripped sarcasm. Arwenna sat up. What time was it? Where was he? Not that she cared, but . . .

'Yes, I'm available.' Her head ached, and she thought she had slept badly, but wasn't awake enough to be sure. 'Aren't you here?'

'If I were, I wouldn't be phoning you,' he answered. 'I went out at ten and I shall be out all day. There's a message for you from Zack by the phone in the lounge. If you want to work I've left some letters out for you to translate. I'll be in about six. Any questions?'

'No.' She put her hand to her aching forehead. 'Oh— where are you if I need you?'

'I doubt you will, but I've left my number by the phone. Don't call unless it's important. Goodbye.' The line went dead, and the dialling tone began. She replaced the receiver. She supposed she had better get up. She could hear a distant hum, and when she had put on a dressing gown and gone into the kitchen, found a middle-aged woman there doing the floor with an electric polisher.

'Good morning, madam,' the woman, said, switching off the machine and smiling at her politely as if she was quite used to seeing strange young women appearing at midday clad in nightclothes. 'I hope this didn't wake you?'

'No.' She probably *was* quite used to it, thought Arwenna. The woman had a pleasant face, grey hair, an efficient manner. She wore a blue nylon smock with 'Frensham Mansions' embroidered on the top pocket.

'I'm Mrs Holt,' the woman added. 'Would you like me to make you a drink, madam?'

'That's very kind of you, Mrs Holt,' Arwenna answered. 'I'd love a coffee. Are you having one as well?' She sat down at the table. 'I'll keep out of your way.'

'I've done in here, anyway. The other rooms are finished. There's only your bedroom, if you wouldn't mind?'

'No, of course not. I'm sorry, I——' Arwenna smiled at her. Mrs Holt was filling a kettle, getting out two cups and saucers, moving quietly and efficiently. The kitchen shone with cleanliness, everything neat and tidy.

'I will have a coffee if you don't mind, madam. Mr Vanner never minds, but I do try to keep out of his way, of course.' She looked at Arwenna. 'Would you like something to eat as well?'

'No, thanks. I've some clothes I must wash. Is there anywhere to dry them?'

'We have a laundry room, madam. Just leave anything out and I'll see they're returned today.'

'Oh, I can do them. It's only lingerie—I just wondered about drying.'

'No trouble at all, madam,' the woman insisted. 'I'll do them personally.' She made the coffee and put it on the table, then went out, to return with a blue plastic bag. 'Pop them in there, and I'll bring it back later.'

'You're very kind. Do sit down.' Arwenna sipped her coffee and Mrs Holt sat down at the table and picked up her cup. 'How often do you come here, Mrs Holt?'

'Three days a week, madam, Monday, Wednesday and Friday. Two other women come as well, and we generally have everything done about noon. But I stayed on to do your room when you'd woken.'

'You should have knocked!' protested Arwenna, dismayed.

'Oh, no, Mr Vanner said not to disturb you.'

'But I wouldn't want to delay you. I'm awfully sorry.'

'Not at all, madam, there was plenty to do in here anyway. You haven't delayed me at all. I believe there's a message for you by the phone,' added Mrs Holt.

'Yes, Mr Vanner called me just now to tell me, otherwise I'm afraid I'd have still been asleep.' She gave a wry grin. 'But I don't make a habit of oversleeping, I assure you. It won't happen again.'

The woman thawed slightly. Her manner had been very formal, but it was as if Arwenna's natural warmth had reached her. 'It's quite all right,' she said. 'Really, it is. And it's no trouble to me. I'd have come back later if necessary. We'd all do anything for Mr Vanner.'

'Are you employed here at the flats full time?'

'Yes. But Mr Vanner gets special treatment, of course.'

Arwenna didn't understand the 'of course'. Why? 'Oh, why? Because this is the penthouse apartment, you mean?'

'Why, no, madam,' the woman looked faintly surprised. 'I mean because of him owning the flats.'

It was Arwenna's turn to look more than faintly surprised. 'Owning? You mean—the whole block?'

'Yes, madam. Didn't you know?'

Arwenna shook her head. She couldn't believe it. 'No. I thought—just this one,' she said at last, stunned.

'Oh, no, it's owned by one of his companies. We're all employed by him. He's a real gentleman too.'

She could have been saying that simply out of politeness—and a shrewd desire to keep well in with the boss—but Arwenna sensed the genuine respect in her voice. 'I'm sure he is,' she said, because there was no way she could say anything else. She had finished her coffee, and it was obvious that Mrs Holt wanted to get on with her work. Arwenna stood up. 'I'll get my things to wash, then I'll work in the main lounge while you do my room.' She picked up the plastic bag.

'Thank you.' Mrs Holt stood as well, and took the cup. 'I'll be done in half an hour.'

Minutes later, Arwenna was sitting in the lounge going through the work that Garth had left. The surprise was fading. She wondered why he hadn't told her. Perhaps he assumed she knew—perhaps he didn't care, either way. But it made her realise something very sharply: how far apart their worlds really were. She had always lived a life where luxuries were to be saved for—never poor, but never rich. She had never wanted more, never felt deprived, and was happy thus. She wondered if Garth was happy, despite all his vast riches. She didn't envy him his wealth; she had never envied anyone anything in her life. There seemed something wrong to her about one person having so much, but she had never really considered it before. There were other things far more important in life than the pursuit of wealth.

She sighed, then dismissed the subject from her mind and got on with the work before her.

When Mrs Holt had gone, she showered and dressed in her most feminine dress, an Indian cotton with swirling design, soft and full; telephoned Zack, who was having a day off to revise for exams, and arranged to meet him the following day, Saturday. They discussed the party, and he made her laugh, and he was warm and caring and human, and she loved him like a brother. She had a brief moment of feeling sorry for Garth, who didn't love anybody, then remembered something. 'Zack,' she said, 'I know you know everything about London. I'm going out tonight with the man you fondly call Thingy—and I'd like to get a nice dress to wear. Any ideas?'

'From me? You're kidding! When do you think *I* last bought a dress?'

'I didn't mean that, idiot. Come on, you know loads of girls. Where's the in place for super dresses at super cheap prices?'

'There's only one girl in my life, honey, and I'm talking to her now. You're serious?'

'Yes, I'm serious.'

'Okay. Get a pencil and paper.' He gave her directions, the addresses of three shops in the Hampstead area, off the beaten track, asked her if she wanted him to go with her, and she thanked him and said no, he'd got work to do, and anyway, she didn't have much time and they'd be talking too much and she'd see him tomorrow anyway. They said their goodbyes and Arwenna hung up and looked from her list to the work she had to do.

If she went now, and took a taxi, she could be back in a couple of hours; it was nearly two. She would work hard from four to six, then be able to get ready. She had already done a lot, and there wasn't much left to do. She wanted to look nice for their evening out at Bill Chisholm's, though she wasn't sure why it seemed so important, except that an intrusive and annoying memory kept coming back, of a girl flinging her arms round Garth's neck and kissing him, in a tiny kitchen, and it refused to go away.

Decided, she picked up the telephone and rang down to the lobby of the flats. Ten minutes later she was on her way.

The door opened, and Garth came in. Arwenna looked up from her notepad, smiled a cool little smile and said hello—then caught her breath.

He nodded. 'Any messages for me?' He looked tired, in need of a shave, and he wore an eye-patch over his left eye, which shocked Arwenna immensely. She stood up and walked towards him, face anxious.

'What's the matter?' she asked.

'You should know. You did it,' he answered, and lifted aside the patch and took it off. 'I got fed up with people asking if I'd walked into a bloody door, if you must know.'

She closed her eyes, seeing only too clearly the glorious hues of the fully developed black eye that stared back accusingly at her. 'Let me do something,' she said quietly. 'Please.'

'Such as? Giving me another one to match? Thanks. I'm sure that'd help a lot.'

'No. I meant—well, what Aunt Daisy said. You've got potatoes, and apples——'

'It's a black eye, not a fruit salad,' he snapped, and sank down on to the settee.

'Let me get you a drink,' she said, and went to the cupboard.

'That's a better idea.' He flexed his hands. 'Make it a whisky—straight.'

She poured him one and handed it to him, and he drank it down in one. He looked as though he needed it. Arwenna's calm, contented mood vanished. She had worked well, and done all he had left, and she had bought a beautiful matching skirt and blouse top that hadn't cost the earth, and she had been feeling good, and happy. Now she felt wretched instead. She felt guilty and unhappy, even as though she were to blame for Garth's obvious tiredness. She wanted to soothe and comfort him, and was disturbed at her own reaction. It was six o'clock, and they would probably leave about seven, to visit Aunt Daisy—on whom she had found time to call that afternoon, having found the clothes in the first shop on Zack's list—and she was going to help Garth in some way, if only to assuage her guilt. She took his glass from him, poured in some more whisky, but not much, and gave it to him, then knelt at his feet. 'Please. Just let me try,' she said. 'You look tired.'

'I am tired—I've been working hard. I'm also quite tough, Arwenna. After a shave and a shower I'll be fine. I'll still have a black eye, but we can't have everything, can we?' His voice was hard. She stayed where she was, and looked at him.

'If you want to insult me, go ahead,' she answered. 'I deserve it.'

'You mean you'll *let* me! *Thanks.*' His tone was heavy with irony. 'I wouldn't know where to start, would I? We'd never get out. All right, go and grate an apple, or whatever you want to do. I'll be in my room.' He finished the drink and handed her the glass. Arwenna took it into the kitchen and rinsed it, found an apple, peeled it, then grated it into a cereal dish. She paused outside Garth's door, hearing a shower running, then knocked. She had never ever been inside it.

'Come in, I'll not be a minute,' he called. She opened the door and went in. His bathroom door was closed, and the water stopped as she entered. She looked around. He had a large antique wardrobe and matching chest of drawers, beautifully polished and old. The bed was large and had a deep brown bedspread over it, matching curtains and furniture. There were several prints on the walls, of vintage cars. It was a very masculine room. Garth walked out wearing only trousers, a towel draped round his shoulders. 'I'll lie on the bed,' he said, 'and you can do your stuff. And while it's setting, or whatever it's supposed to do, I'd appreciate it if you'd make me a cup of coffee. Black, strong, no sugar.'

'Yes,' she answered. He lay down and she sat beside him. She had mashed the grated apple as finely as she could and it was turning faintly brown. Garth closed his eyes and she leaned over and applied the mushy mixture carefully round his eye. He didn't move a muscle.

'And how long,' he asked, when she stood up, 'do I have to stay like this?'

'About ten minutes.' She fled. She was mad, she knew she was. She made his coffee and took it back. Garth lay perfectly still, eyes closed. He could have been asleep.

'Do you want to drink it now?' she asked quietly.

'How? On my back?'

'No, I'll lift your head. Look, let me put this towel round you——' she did so, 'then if any mush falls off it won't go on the bed. There now.' She reached over and slipped her hand behind his head. 'Gently does it.' He let her. He suddenly seemed to be quite pliant and unresisting. He opened his good eye as she eased his head quietly up, and gave her a baleful glance. Ignoring it, she put the coffee cup to his mouth. He drank some, then said:

'That's enough.' Arwenna eased him back again and looked at her watch. Ten minutes were nearly up.

'I'll go and get a washcloth and a dish,' she told him, and went to get them.

'How does it feel?' she asked when she returned. 'Any better?'

'No.' She sighed and began cleansing the poultice off. What had she expected? A miracle? Two minutes later all was cleared and she looked closely at his eye as he sat up. It looked very much the same as it had before. He touched it carefully. 'Mmm,' he said. 'Soothing. It's not gone, has it?' This in dry tones.

'I'm afraid not. But I'll do it again later.'

Garth swung his legs over the side of the bed and she moved away. 'I shouldn't bother,' he remarked. 'It'll go, eventually.'

'Garth,' she bit her lip, 'I'm—sorry.'

He removed a minute portion of apple from his

arm. 'Yes, I know. You already said.' He looked at her. 'You're quite something, you know that? Really something. I've never had a black eye in my life before, and I've been in some scraps when I was younger. And you come along into my life and put your mark on me straight away. I must be mad!'

'So you must. You talk as though I forced my way in. Listen—it was you, not me, remember?'

'I'll never forget,' he retorted dryly. 'I'll certainly never forget you as long as I live. And don't start with the smart answers. The new you—the one I met fifteen minutes ago with an anxious face, who couldn't do enough for me—"let me get you a drink"'—he added, in fair imitation of her tones, 'is okay for a while longer. It's quite a change from the firecracker I've come to know and love over the past few days——' He stopped, as if suddenly aware of what he had said, but the words didn't register with Arwenna, not then. She was too incensed at his mimicry of her voice at that moment.

'Firecracker!' she exploded. 'Me? If I'm a firecracker, what the hell are you?' She put her hands on her hips. 'I've been working hard all afternoon for you, *and* I nipped out and bought a dress because you wanted me to for tonight *and* I paid for the taxi myself, *and* bought the dress with my own money, and I've already said I'm sorry for hitting you, and you deserved it anyway. You seem to forget *that*, and I don't intend to go on apologising for the rest of my life, and you make me sick——' She stopped. What was that he had said? 'The firecracker I've come to know and love——' 'And *love*?' Him? What a stupid, ridiculous thing to have said!

Garth sat down suddenly again on the bed and put his head in his hands, leaning forward as if in pain, and Arwenna's anger faded away as quickly as it had come. She knelt down, heart beating fast at the sight of him, suddenly so still, as if ill. 'Garth?' Then, as he didn't answer, she put her hands out tentatively and touched him on the shoulders. 'Garth, are you all right?' she asked anxiously. Her heart hammered in sudden fear, and her mouth was dry.

He nodded, and made a sound, more like a groan, but stayed where he was. Was he ill? 'Please speak,' she whispered.

'Just go away and leave me alone,' he said, very quietly, but with intensity.

'No. Not while you're like—are you in pain?' She sat beside him on the bed. She was shivering.

'No. Leave me——' He seemed to be trembling.

'Garth——'

'Get out. For God's sake—get *out*,' he muttered, and there was such terrible violence in the words that she jumped to her feet as if to escape him, and stood there poised, torn with indecision. Then he looked up at her, and she was frightened at what she saw. She didn't understand it, and that was worse, and she couldn't move. Then he got to his feet and put his hand out to her arm. His fingers, when he held her arm, were hard, almost biting into the flesh. 'I want you out of my room,' he grated. 'Don't you understand?' He took his fingers away as if she had burned him. Sure that he had some sudden, awful fever, Arwenna took a step forward to him and held out her hands.

'I can't leave you——' she began, 'not like——' He swung his left arm out, striking away the hands she was holding towards him, to help him, and, stunned by the violence, she staggered back, clasping her wrist where his hand had struck her, gasping with the shock of it. Then, turning, physically frightened, she ran out, and along to her room. Inside she stood shaking by the door, rubbing her wrist. Garth had landed out blindly, and she felt the burning sensation where his hand had met her wrist, and felt almost sick with shock.

The door opened and he was there. She whirled round, hand going to her throat in an instinctive gesture of self-protection. 'Arwenna,' he said, 'Oh God, forgive me Arwenna—I didn't mean——'

'Don't touch me again,' she whispered. 'I left— I got out——'

'I didn't know what I was doing—I didn't intend to hurt you, I swear it. I only——' he stopped. There was agony on his face, and in his eyes. 'I couldn't see —I was telling you to go——' He walked slowly towards her, hands held out, palms upward. 'Dear God, I wouldn't strike you—I wouldn't ever *knowingly* hit *you.*'

'You did,' she gasped. 'You hurt my hand—see?' She held it up, and he took it, and bent his face to it and kissed it. Then slowly, as if compelled by a force stronger than he knew, he put his arms around her, trembling as if indeed he were in the grip of a fever, and held her to him tightly.

'Please forgive me,' he said, and his voice was broken and husky. 'Please forgive me—I didn't intend that——'

'All right, I forgive you,' she whispered. 'I know you didn't mean to hit me—I know it was accidental. I only thought you were ill, that's all—I only wanted to help.' She felt the tremor of his body against hers. 'Are you sure you're all right?'

'I am now.' He put his hand up to her chin and tilted her face slightly upwards, and she knew he was going to kiss her a moment before he did so. It was a strangely gentle kiss, a kiss that followed on his asking for forgiveness; it had neither passion nor excitement, but a longing for reassurance, and she had never known anything so very beautiful in her life. She responded to it, putting her hands behind his shoulder to hold him to her. They blended, they melted as though become one, and in his great strength was a gentleness she had also never known.

When the kiss was over, Garth held her against his heart, so that she felt the beats in her head, and heard, over that sound, his voice as he said: 'We'd better get ready if we're to leave soon.'

'Yes, I know.' But she didn't move, and neither did he. There was no explanation for her wanting to stay in his arms after all that had happened, but she did.

'Your aunt will be expecting us.'

'Yes, she will.' But neither moved. Garth wasn't trembling now, neither was Arwenna. She felt only a great welling of strength from him, as though her whole body was getting a charge, almost like electricity. It was wonderful and very satisfying, and she wanted it to go on and on ...

She heard his deep sigh, almost a groan, but not of pain. They stood there in the sunlit room, and it might have been for seconds or minutes. There was no count of time at all. She only knew a complete and utter sensation of well being and happiness. At last, and as if by mutual consent, and at the same moment they moved slightly away from each other, and looked into each other's eyes. Garth gave a faint smile. 'If you feel like I do,' he said, 'you'll feel ready for anything. I feel as though I've just had my batteries recharged.'

'So do I,' she admitted. He touched her face with the back of his hand.

'I'm sorry, I should have shaved first. Your cheeks are very pink.'

'Are they? Never mind.' It seemed an inane conversation, but some things can never be said. 'They'll match my outfit. Which reminds me, I'd better get it on.'

'Yes,' he said. 'Let me see it.'

Arwenna walked away and opened her wardrobe and took it out.

CHAPTER TEN

It was as though a truce had been declared, and one that was to be scrupulously observed by both sides. Arwenna held out the skirt and slim-fitting blouse in pale pink, silky material, fine knit, and was pleased herself with it. Garth touched the pleated skirt. 'Very attractive,' he commented. 'Harrod's?'

She smiled. 'No. A little shop—a boutique on the borders of Hampstead. I saw it, tried it on, and bought it. Twenty minutes and I was on my way back h——' She was about to say 'home' and substituted, 'here.'

'Clever. And quick. I approve.' The atmosphere, over the last few moments, had completely changed. As though something was safely locked away inside them both, hidden, both aware—the awareness was in the air—but calmness on the surface. For how long? thought Arwenna. It must stay like this, like it is, civilised and pleasant, or we will destroy each other— or he will destroy me.

The explosive, devastating scene of before, which had led to the embrace, which in turn had led to this safe haven, had been too shattering for words. Life could not hold too many of those, and there had been enough in just a brief few days to last nearly a lifetime. She took both skirt and blouse off the hanger and laid them on the bed. 'If you'd be kind enough to unbutton me at the back before you go,' she told him, 'I'd appreciate it. I can do it—but only with a bit of arm-stretching.' And I don't feel strong enough, she added, but silently.

'Of course. Turn round.' She did so and he unbuttoned the dozen or so tiny buttons with care. 'Okay?'

'Yes, thanks.' She turned to face him again.

150

'Sure you can manage now?' A slight smile, no more aggression, just a mild joke that she could appreciate.

'Oh yes, I think so.' A little smile back, just to let him know.

He shrugged. 'Well, I tried.' He went towards the door. 'Fifteen minutes enough for you?'

'If you go now.'

He went out. Arwenna let out her breath in a silent and deep sigh, and took off her dress. Let the truce continue, she thought. Please let it continue.

They spent a pleasant evening at the Chisholms' elegant house, after visiting Aunt Daisy, and it was nearly twelve-thirty when they arrived back at the apartment. There had been only the four of them, and Ann Chisholm had prepared a fantastic buffet supper that had made Arwenna realise, belatedly, that she had eaten very little all day. Garth was as much at home in their house as he had been the previous night at Steve and Zack's party, and had moreover, been charming and considerate to Arwenna. The truce continued and flourished, and on the way back she dozed off in the car, so totally relaxed and exhausted was she.

She was awoken by his voice: 'Wake up, sleepyhead, we're home,' and opened her eyes to see they were parked by the lift.

'Good heavens, did I fall asleep?' she gasped.

'You did.' He leaned over and opened her door. 'Out you get.'

Waking up rapidly, she stumbled out and stood on the hard concrete, waiting while he locked the doors, then led her to the lift. 'Straight to bed for you,' he said.

'Are we working in the morning?' she asked, as they sped upwards. 'I'm sorry I overslept today, truly. I'll make up for it over the weekend.'

'We'll talk about work in the morning, not now.'
He closed the lift door behind them, then they were
inside his apartment. Garth loosened his tie and
yawned. 'I'm pretty tired myself,' he said. He had
switched on only one lamp, and the soft light was
sufficient.

'I had a lovely evening,' she told him. 'Thank you
for taking me.'

'So did I. You looked very elegant in that outfit.'

'Did I? Thank you.' She slipped off her high-heeled
sandals and gave a sigh. 'That's better.' Carrying them,
she walked towards her bedroom. 'Goodnight, Garth.'

'Goodnight.'

Arwenna fell straightaway into a deep sleep the
minute her head touched the pillow, and woke several
hours later, wide awake, alert, as she heard a faint
sound from somewhere near. She looked at her bedside
clock, which showed nearly five-thirty. It was just getting light outside, and very early bird sounds came
faintly through her open window. Arwenna sat up in
bed and threw the covers aside and crept to the door.
She opened it very quietly, then heard the noise again.
It seemed to be coming from the kitchen, although the
door was closed. The faintest bang, as of a cupboard
shutting. She waited a moment, and heard a strange
fluttering sound which sent a chill up her spine.

Quickly, quietly, she ran into Garth's bedroom, put
her hand to his mouth, and shook him. As he woke up
she leaned over, keeping her hand pressed over his
mouth, and whispered:

'There's someone in the kitchen.'

He was instantly awake. He nodded and sat up,
grabbing a dressing gown as he did so. Arwenna turned
her head away, just in case ...

'Stay there,' he whispered, and went out. There was
no way she was not going with him, and she crept out
after him, saw him open the kitchen door and switch

the lights on. She nearly collided with him as he turned in the doorway and started to laugh

'What——' she began, and peered round him to see a very frightened blackbird scrabbling frantically up the window trying to get out. 'Oh!'

'Someone left the window open,' he said, and she remembered opening the small top window that afternoon. 'Shut the door. I'll get it out.'

She did so, and Garth went and opened the larger window below, and the grateful bird dived out and vanished. He closed them both firmly.

'I'm sorry,' she said. 'It was me.'

'No great harm done. Well——' as he looked around, 'not much.'

'I'll get a cloth,' she said, and opened the cupboard beneath the sink.

'And I'll make coffee. Want one?'

'Please.' She began busily wiping away at the various small souvenirs of the bird's visit. 'Poor thing must have been here all night.'

'Weren't you scared when it woke you?'

'No.' She looked up at him. 'I thought it might just be you at first, until I heard a fluttery noise that sent a shiver right through me. Then I woke you.'

He produced two beakers and made the coffee. 'Most women would have screamed for help.'

'What, and frighten the burglar away? I thought you'd rather catch him.' She sipped her coffee. 'I'm wide awake now.' She sighed. 'With oversleeping yesterday I won't get to sleep again. I might as well stay up and do some work.'

'You've got to be joking!' said Garth, and looked at her as though she was mad.

'No, I'm not.' She smiled. 'Honestly. I often used to get up at home about six and go for a long walk.'

'You're *quite* mad!'

Arwenna had a sudden surge of pure, undiluted

happiness. It was one of those rare flashes that come totally without reason or warning. It was a good-to-be-alive sensation, filling her, making her face glow, and she saw his eyes change as he watched her, and laughed.

'I'm *not*! In fact, I think I'll get dressed and go out and walk for miles!'

Garth drank his coffee much as he had done the whisky the previous night—as if he needed it. 'The door's double locked. I won't let you out.'

'Try and stop me! Get dressed and come with me. Go on, it'll do you good.'

He gazed at her as though he wasn't believing what he was seeing. 'You really mean it, don't you?'

'Yes.'

'Then so help me, I must be crazy as well.' He stood up. 'Go on, then.'

'You'll do it?'

He nodded. 'I want my head examined, but yes, I'll do it.'

'See you in five minutes.' Arwenna ran to her room, stripped, washed, dressed in comfortable jeans and sweater, grabbed her coat, and went into the lounge to wait. All was still outside, the city about to wake up, but not yet ready. It would be an interesting experience, to see it when everyone was still abed. She turned as Garth appeared, wearing jeans and dark blue sweater. He scowled at her. 'Change your mind?'

'No.' She shook her head. 'Come on.'

He took his key out of his pocket, muttered something, and unlocked the door, carrying a dark suede jacket.

They crept out of the car park like two burglars, and set off walking down the silent street. Garth put his jacket on when they had rounded the corner, and Arwenna slipped her arm in his. 'Smile,' she said.

'Later I might. I'm not awake yet,' he responded. There was a distant whine, and an electric milk float appeared, crates rattling on the back. It stopped, and the milkman jumped out and vanished into the doorway of a block of flats, and they walked past, and on to a main road. Cars were passing, not many of them, but a few; two men were cycling to work, one whistling as they passed. A cat dived down basement steps when it saw them, and watched them suspiciously from the door at the bottom.

They passed banks, and travel agents and shops, most with faint lights burning inside, and in the distance was the sound of heavier traffic and a train from far away. After they had walked for what seemed like miles they were nearing Euston Station and Arwenna said: 'Come on, let's go in and see what's happening.'

Garth looked at her, and shook his head as if he wasn't sure what was happening to him; they ran up the steps at the side, and along, and into the main entrance. Their footsteps echoed hollowly on the shiny stone floor, where a few people wandered about waiting for trains to arrive or depart, and several pigeons landed hopefully nearby. A policeman eyed them suspiciously, then walked away, and Garth said: 'If we get arrested, I shall blame you *entirely*, I want you to know that,' and Arwenna answered:

'I've never been arrested. I wonder what it feels like?' He grabbed her arm firmly, then took hold of her hand and held it as if he would never let her go.

'Come on,' he said, 'let's go back. I'm a respectable citizen and if you dare break any windows I shall deny I know you.'

She laughed, and kissed him, and he looked startled. 'What was that for?' he demanded.

'Because the policeman's looking, so you won't be able to deny it,' she said. He stopped walking, took her in his arms, and kissed her soundly, to the interested speculation of two women cleaners walking wearily past towards the platforms.

'What was that for?' she asked, and knew quite suddenly that she loved him with all her heart, and wondered why she hadn't realised before what was happening to her.

'Nothing. Just to shut you up,' he answered.

They walked out. Arwenna was silent now, and when Garth flagged down a passing taxi she made no protest. She had just discovered something very disturbing and frightening, and it had shaken her so much that she didn't know how she would ever look at him again without giving herself away. She sat back in the taxi and thought, oh dear, I wish it hadn't happened. I wish I hadn't woken up—but it would have happened later if not then, she knew. It hurt. I didn't know it would be like this, she thought. I didn't know it would be like a pain inside, an ache——

'You're very quiet,' he commented, and she saw that they were back at the car park, and had left the taxi and were walking towards the lift.

'Yes,' she answered. 'I'm sorry, I should never have dragged you out so early,' and as he opened the lift doors she burst into tears, and was horrified, but couldn't stop herself.

Garth led her into the apartment, closed the door, and put his arm round her. 'What on earth's the matter?' he asked, sounding quite shaken.

Sobbing helplessly, she couldn't even begin to attempt an answer, and what did she say, anyway? How could she tell a man who had admitted that he wanted an affair with her, simply to get her out of his system, that she had gone and done something utterly stupid like falling head over heels in love with him? She didn't. Or she was asking for trouble. There had been enough trouble already, when she hadn't even liked him. And as far as Garth was concerned she would be just another woman in a long line stretching back, and forward, to infinity.

He sat her down firmly on the settee and sat beside her, and began to rub her hands as if they were cold, as they might have been, for all she knew. 'Please stop,' he said. 'Please—Arwenna, stop crying.' He sounded very fraught, not at all the man in command, and she hiccuped, and stopped crying, startled at that strange phenomenon. Garth—fraught?

'Thank God,' he muttered. 'Look, was it something I said?'

She shook her head and sniffed, and he produced a neatly ironed handkerchief and said: 'Blow your nose,' so she did so.

'Can I get you a drink?' he asked. 'A cup of tea?'

'N-o——' Her voice was faint, almost a squeak. He sighed, and sat back as if she had exhausted him.

'Can you tell me what made you cry?'

She shook her head. Garth stood up and looked down at her for a moment. She had her head down and could only see his shoes, and she kept her eyes fixed firmly on them. The next moment he was kneeling before her, lifting her chin, so that she had to look at him. She swallowed hard.

'All right,' he said gently, 'I won't ask again. Would you like to go and lie down? It's not eight yet.'

'No, I'm all right now.' She gave a tremulous smile. She had to start now. *Now*, before he could guess anything, before he could see. He must never know, or she would be lost. 'I'll make breakfast, and then, if you'll give me some work, I'll get started.'

'If you think that's best, fine.' He was obviously going to agree with anything she said. Men were supposed, traditionally, to be frightened by a woman's tears, but she hadn't thought it would have had this effect on him.

She dabbed at her cheeks, tucked the handkerchief away in her pocket, and stood up. Garth stood watching her as if she might break into pieces if he moved too suddenly. She took a deep breath. When she walked out she glanced back. He was lighting a cheroot, and he looked as though he had just been hit very hard.

Arwenna worked all morning. Garth had gone out about nine, saying that he would be back for lunch, and did she want him to fetch something to eat, or make lunch himself, or would she?

She said she would make something, and what would he like, and he assured her that absolutely anything would do, and was she sure she was all right? After being assured that she was, he left. She worked hard until noon, then stopped to prepare food. She was meeting Zack at four, and was visiting Aunt Daisy before that. Apart from telling her that he would call in and see Aunt Daisy during the morning, Garth had not told her where he was going.

During the morning's work it had been easy to not think about her feelings for Garth. Preparing the meal in the kitchen it was no longer possible to keep the thoughts from crowding in. She longed to see him again—and she dreaded it, both at the same time; a difficult mixture. The intercom telephone rang in the kitchen as she was making a cheese sauce to go with the marrow she had prepared. It was Fred, the day-time doorman, to tell her that a friend of Mr Vanner's was wanting to come up.

'He's not here at the moment,' she told him. 'Who is it?'

'A Mr Spence—he's a frequent visitor, madam,' Fred answered. 'Says it's important.'

'Mr Vanner will be back soon. Please send him up, will you?'

'Right you are, madam.'

She hung up. She had no way of contacting Garth. He hadn't left a number. She took off her apron as the door buzzed and went to let the unknown visitor in.

A tall attractive man stood there, sober-suited, fair-haired, blue-eyed. He smiled, looking faintly puzzled. 'Good morning, I'm sorry to call in like this, but I do need to see Garth quite soon. Will it be convenient for me to wait? My name's Jason Spence, and I'm an old friend of his.'

'Yes, do come in, Mr Spence. I'm Arwenna Holmes. I'm just preparing lunch at the moment. I'm sorry, but I don't know where Garth is, but he should be in soon.'

'Can I help?' He followed her through to the kitchen before she could say yes or no, and seated himself at the table. Arwenna looked at him in some amusement as she put her apron back on again.

'Not unless you want to peel potatoes?' she grinned, looking at the immaculate grey suit.

'Fair enough.' He stood up and took off his jacket and laid it neatly over the back of the chair. 'Got a spare apron?'

'Good heavens, I was joking!' she exclaimed.

He looked at her, as amused as she was. 'I'm not.'

'You've got yourself a job.' She found a tea towel and he draped it round his waist with the air of a master chef donning an apron.

Arwenna stirred the cheese into the blended sauce and left it to be heated later, checked the steak simmering gently in a wine sauce. It smelt delicious, as did the mushrooms.

She prepared the marrow as he peeled three large potatoes, then said: 'If you'd like to stay to lunch, you'd better do a couple more. They're in the rack over there.'

'That's extremely kind of you.' He looked pleased.

'It's no trouble. You say you're an old friend of Garth's. Do you live in London?'

'No, Colchester. I came up last night, intended to phone, and got tied up. So, as I was passing, I called in instead. He has been known to be in on a Saturday morning.'

But not after silly women like me burst into tears, she thought. 'He won't be long now.'

'Are you an—er—old friend of Garth's?' he enquired with some delicacy. He wasn't making a bad job of peeling the potatoes into the sink with the waste disposal unit either.

'Not really. I'm working for him. And my aunt's had an operation at the clinic of his friend Bill Chisholm. Do you know him?'

'Oh, Bill! Of course! I introduced them seven—oh —eight years ago.'

That was a conversational opener if ever there was one. Arwenna told Jason about the previous evening's visit there, and they discovered almost instantaneously that they got on very well with each other. Jason was extremely funny, a witty raconteur, and one topic led to another, and they were deep in conversation over two glasses of sherry in the kitchen, supervising the cooking at the same time, and Arwenna's laughter pealed out just after Jason finished telling her about a disastrous holiday he had once had in Austria, when Garth walked in.

They looked round, startled, Jason leaning well back, sprawling in the chair, long legs under the table, jacketless, tea towel-clad, laughing helplessly—seeing Garth at the same moment that Arwenna did.

'Garth!' Jason jumped to his feet, whipping off the tea towel, and the two men shook hands. Garth said :

'I see you two have introduced yourselves,' with a slightly raised eyebrow towards the bottle of best sherry on the table.

'Arwenna's been entertaining me in between letting me do all the work, yes,' said Jason, and gave her a wink. It was difficult to tell Garth's mood. 'And she's invited me to lunch.'

'Good.'

'It's nearly ready. If you men want to talk privately, when would you like it serving?' She prodded the potatoes with a fork. Another five minutes would do it.

'Look, Garth, it'll only take a few minutes,' Jason gave her an apologetic look. 'Will you excuse us for five minutes? No more, I promise.'

'Of course. Five minutes,' she nodded. They went out, and she grinned to herself. That meant ten. She set out mats and cutlery, put plates to warm, and poured herself some sherry.

Everything was ready when she heard them coming back, laughing and talking like the old friends they clearly were. Lunch was splendid. Arwenna was pleased that Jason was there. It smoothed over what might have been a difficult situation, and Jason was excellent company, taking charge of the conversation, as it were. Although Garth was obviously pleased to see him, he seemed fairly thoughtful—at least to Arwenna's sensitive awareness of him.

After they had eaten she excused herself, ostensibly to get ready for the afternoon, in reality to give them an opportunity to talk. Garth had been to see Aunt Daisy, and had returned with some fruit and soft drinks for her. She decided she would go alone, and when she went into the lounge, changed into her favourite blue dress—washed and ironed by the competent Mrs Holt—she told them so. They were sprawled out on the settee, talking quietly. Both men stood up when she went in, and she was aware of Jason's admiring all-encompassing glance.

Garth looked at his watch. 'We'll all go, what say you, Jason? Aunt Daisy's quite a character.'

'Love to.' Jason emptied his glass, and put it down.

'What time are you meeting Zack?' asked Garth.

'Four o'clock outside Foyle's.'

'Zack?' enquired Jason, with an ever so polite smile.

'An old friend,' Arwenna explained, as Garth seemed disinclined to do so.

'Ah. Right, Garth. My day's free—now we've got that little matter sorted out, we'll go off somewhere when we've dropped Arwenna.'

She went to gather up her bag, and the basket of fruit, and Jason rushed to help her. Then they set off to visit the clinic.

Zack was standing outside Foyle's as the car drew up at the curb. Arwenna turned to Jason. 'It was nice meeting you,' she said. 'Goodbye.'

'And you. Thanks for a delicious lunch. I may see you later. *Au revoir*, Arwenna.' She slid out of the car, and Garth leaned over. 'How long will you be out?' he enquired.

'I don't know.' She looked towards Zack, who was crossing the pavement towards them, as the traffic honked behind them, annoyed at Garth stopping. 'About eight?'

'See you then. Take care.' He was gone, the powerful car accelerating swiftly to be swallowed up in the traffic. Zack kissed her.

'Hi, beautiful. Let's have a coffee first, then a wander round, okay?'

'I am in your hands entirely,' she answered.

'Mmm!' he groaned. 'I wish you were, honey.' He took her arm possessively. 'Still with that bloated capitalist, I see.'

'I'm afraid so.' She looked at him as they walked along arm in arm. 'Not jealous, are you?'

'What do you think?' he laughed. 'Insanely jealous, maddened—foaming at the mouth jealous.'

'You're an idiot!'

'I know—I must be. Come on, this place does a nice coffee. Then we'll go and feed the pigeons in Trafalgar Square, then we'll make our way to Hyde Park and stroll among the lovers and perhaps I'll persuade you——'

'No,' she said, laughing. There were never any tensions with Zack. Not like Garth. Easy-going, humourous, he was the ideal companion for Arwenna in her present state. It was so ridiculous to have fallen in love with a man like Garth. She wished she could put him out of her mind, and just enjoy her time with Zack. And that, after a few minutes of his conversation, in wit and humour and warm affection, was precisely what she managed to do.

It was nearer nine than eight when at last, feeling rather tired, she said farewell to Zack. He was going on to a party, and tried to persuade her to go, but she had had a long day, which had caught up on her. He insisted, despite her protestations, on walking with her to the corner of the street where she was staying. 'See you again some time soon, honey,' he said, looking deep into her eyes. 'Be good. Don't do anything I wouldn't do.'

She laughed, and stroked his rough beard. 'I'll try and remember that.'

Zack was holding her hands then. 'Don't fall for him,' he said, and she didn't need to ask whom he meant. 'He'll break your heart. He's the kind who uses women.'

'I know,' she answered softly. But she didn't tell him his advice had come too late. That was her secret— and always would be. 'I'll phone you, Zack, before I go back home. We'll keep in touch as well.'

'Okay, honey. 'Night. Take care!'

'I will.' She watched him lope away, whistling, then turned and began to walk slowly towards the main entrance. Zack was wrong about one thing. The danger from Garth lay not in his attitude to women—but in his dominant personality. She could compete with other women, but she couldn't have her life taken over, and he could easily. Arwenna was too independent-spirited to ever allow that to happen. She loved him. She couldn't help that, but she could help the way she reacted to him, now and in the brief future they had. She ran up the steps, and the evening porter was on duty, reading a paper. He got up when he saw her and went over to the lift.

'Mr Vanner's at home, madam,' he told her.

'Thanks, George.' The lift whisked her up, and she pressed the bell on the door.

Garth opened it, and she could tell by the faint blue haze of cigar smoke, even before she saw Jason, that he wasn't alone. Jason rose to his feet as she walked in. The table was littered with papers, both men were jacketless, and with ties loosened, and two glasses and a bottle of whisky on the table told of a busy evening.

'Hello,' she greeted him.

'I said we'd meet again,' he answered, and grinned. 'Did you have a nice afternoon out?'

'Very pleasant, thanks.' She regarded the table. 'I can see you're busy, so I won't disturb you.'

'We've finished,' Garth answered. 'Haven't we?'

'Yes.' Jason began to gather up the papers. 'Thank God. I've had enough for one day. Come and sit down and talk to me.'

'Want a drink, Arwenna?' Garth asked.

'I'd like a coffee more than anything. May I?'

'Of course.' There was something wrong with Garth. She didn't know what it was, a certain reserve, no more than that.

'Would you both like one?'

'I would,' answered Jason. 'Let me help you.'

He followed her to the kitchen, leaving Garth in the main lounge putting papers away. 'We've not eaten,' he said. 'Have you?'

'No.' She was filling the kettle while he banged about opening cupboard doors. 'Have you been working all this time?'

'Since we left you? Yes.' He laughed. 'You don't know Garth very well, do you?'

'Hardly at all,' she answered dryly. 'If you're hungry I'm sure I could whip something up.'

'If it's as delicious as that lunch, I'd say yes, but let's see what old Garth suggests, shall we? I'm sure you're not here to slave over a hot stove as well as doing all that mound of translating for him. You're quite a girl, aren't you?'

She glanced at him as he passed her three beakers, and his eyes were gently admiring. 'Why, thank you, sir,' she smiled, and gave a little curtsey, and he laughed.

'I'll go and ask him,' he said, and went out. Arwenna made coffee, put it on a tray with milk and sugar, and carried it in. They were talking as she went in and looked round, and Garth came forward to take the tray from her and put it on the now cleared table.

'We're all hungry,' he said, 'so why don't we go out and eat?'

'Not me. I'm too tired,' she answered. 'I'll have a piece of toast and an early night, I think——'

'Nonsense,' Jason cut in. 'It's only nine. You're in London, and the night is young, and so are you. I wouldn't hear of it, and neither would Garth. I've got a much better idea. How are you on a flutter at the tables?'

'Gambling?' she laughed. 'I don't know. I've never done any.' The two men exchanged glances.

'Then that seems to be settled,' said Jason smoothly.

'I'm a member of a very nice club that does excellent food, and has a casino better than any Monte Carlo has to offer. Let's drink our coffee and go.'

Arwenna sat down weakly. 'No,' she began. 'It sounds lovely, but I don't think——'

Jason sat beside her. 'All you have to do is go and change into your prettiest outfit—though you look perfect anyway—we'll go and have a bite, a quick flutter, and then home to bed. What more could a girl want?'

'And you might have beginner's luck,' said Garth.

She looked at them both. Why not? 'All right,' she agreed. 'Thank you.'

'Good.' Jason finished his coffee in one and stood up, rubbing his chin. 'Can I borrow your razor, Garth?'

'Help yourself. You know where everything is.'

Jason went out. Arwenna picked up her beaker and drank her coffee. Now that they were alone, she didn't feel easy. She had been having many thoughts over the past hours, even minutes, and they were rapidly crystallising into something less tenuous. Everything that was happening, and had happened, only served to make her realise that she could not go on much longer staying with, and working for, Garth. She had to get away soon, before it was too late.

He was planning on taking her to France after Aunt Daisy was home. She knew, in the things that had already happened, as though they were clues to a situation, that if she went she would somehow never be free. France was a country for lovers. Here she was strong enough, but there, miles away from home, all would be so different. How would she resist the inevitable? She looked up at Garth, and he was watching her silently, face expressionless. She looked away again, down at the tray on the table, and a shiver ran down her spine.

She knew one thing, it wasn't going to be easy. But with Garth, nothing was.

Not yet. Not yet. There would be the time when it was right to speak. But it wasn't yet. 'And what are you thinking now?' he asked softly.

'Nothing important,' she answered. 'Nothing that can't wait.' She looked up at him again, eyes shining with her new-found inner strength, and saw him catch his breath. It was almost—for a moment—as if he knew. He couldn't, of course, but she would have to be careful. There were many things to be considered, very many things, before she made the break. 'I'll go and get ready,' she said, and stood up and walked away from him. It seemed somehow symbolic of what was to come.

CHAPTER ELEVEN

THEY took a taxi to the casino, the three of them, Arwenna and Garth and Jason. Arwenna had put on her new pink suit, her highest heeled sandals, and carried a warm white stole. She had opened the envelope and taken out of it ten pounds and put that in her purse. She would gamble some of that, no more. She had no idea then how high the stakes were ...

The place was full when they went in, and as they crossed the crowded lounge to the restaurant she saw the three of them in a wide wall mirror—she between the two men, tall, yet overshadowed by them both. Garth and Jason were well over six feet, Garth slightly the taller of the two, and the picture they made was impressive, even in this place of wealth, and golden, elegant men and women. The mirror image was to remain in her mind for a long time afterwards, and she was aware that others looked at them, and remained looking, and some smiled in recognition, and were

greeted in return. She felt like a princess, and smiled
inwardly at this small conceit, but it was pleasant to
feel so, even if only for a while.

They were escorted into a discreetly lit small dining
room, and Jason ordered champagne, and Arwenna
studied an ornate menu while a waiter hovered by,
pencil and pad poised. She ordered smoked salmon,
and scampi with salad. The champagne arrived, and
by the time her smoked salmon came she had had
several glasses and was feeling decidedly happy and
relaxed. No longer tired either, amazingly, but wide
awake. Both men were good company—no tension
with Garth now. He too seemed totally relaxed. She
loved him so much that just to be with him was both
bliss and pain. She knew what she was going to have
to do, but that was in the future, and now was now, so
she lived for the moment, glowing with the inner
warmth she felt, and more than one pair of male eyes
lingered on her—a fact not unnoticed by either man.

She was practically floating by the end of the meal,
when they entered yet another darker room filled with
tables, and silent intent people. It was a whole new
world to Arwenna, whose only knowledge of casinos
had been via television and films. This was real. The
smoke drifted and hung wreathed about the lights over
the tables. Roulette, blackjack, chemin-de-fer—all was
fascinating. She looked at the serious faces round the
tables, piles of chips at their side, heard the voices of
the croupiers at the roulette table as they stood by
one, quiet and watchful. '*Merci, mesdames et mes-
sieurs, faites vos jeux* ...'

Jason moved away. When he returned, he held a
stack of plastic coins, and handed Arwenna several.
'Go on,' he said softly, 'have a go.'

'But I——' she began, and was shushed by an
elderly dowager by her side.

He whispered: 'Watch this game. See where they place the chips. Watch.'

'All right,' she mouthed. She observed, saw the chips placed in various parts of the numbered green baize, watched the ball click-clicking round the moving wheel, then the croupier's long-handled rake raking in, then giving to others. Simple, it looked, but she still hadn't a clue how the winnings were worked out.

She leaned over and placed three of the chips on number three, for no reason except that she might as well start somewhere.

She didn't realise that she had won until Garth put his hand on her arm. 'Beginner's luck,' he whispered in her ear, and Arwenna, rather dazed, gathered up a pile of chips and stared at them.

'Mine?' she gasped.

Jason took her away from the table, away from the annoyed dowager. 'You've just won three hundred pounds, my dear girl,' he told her.

'What!' She looked at them. '*How* much?'

'Three hundred,' he said. 'Told you. How are you on pontoon?'

'The card game? Do they play it here?'

'Something like it. It's called blackjack. Come on.' He led her over to a horseshoe-shaped table and sat her down, remaining behind her. Garth had disappeared. Dazed, Arwenna took a card, following Jason's whispered instructions, and some half hour later had won nearly a thousand pounds.

She couldn't believe it. Totally bewildered, she sat at a quiet corner table and looked at the chips before her. Garth stood there, silent. It was Jason to whom she spoke. It was almost as though he were not with them. Jason handed her a glass of champagne. 'Drink that,' he ordered.

'I need it—thanks. This money's yours,' she added,

'not mine. I can't believe my luck, but I don't want to play any more.'

'Very sensible, but may I ask why?'

She shrugged. 'I don't know. It's not for fear of losing, not that, because it's like pretend money as far as I'm concerned—it's not *real*, you know. I've just decided, I'm not really a gambler. I've enjoyed coming here very much, and I wouldn't have missed it for anything, but it's over now.' She handed him the pile of multicoloured discs. 'Thanks.'

'You little idiot! *You* won it, it's yours. Pay me back what I started you with if you must, but what you won is yours.' He looked at his watch. 'What say we have another bottle of champagne and then go?'

Garth nodded. 'You'll stay the night, of course?'

'I was hoping you'd ask. Yes, I will.' He took the chips and left, and a moment later a waiter appeared with a bottle of champagne in a bucket.

'Did you gamble?' asked Arwenna.

'I lost a few pounds at roulette, that's all. I rarely gamble. Jason's keener than I am.' He sipped the champagne thoughtfully. 'But you're not, I take it?'

'No, it's been fun, but quite enough to last me for a lifetime. The money I won—it's not mine. I shan't let Jason give it to me.'

'It's yours. He staked you, that's all. If you'd have lost do you think he'd have demanded his money back?'

'No, but——'

'Well then, it's yours. Take it.' Garth looked away as if the subject was closed. Arwenna stared hard at him, trying to understand the way his mind worked. That was impossible. Perhaps he didn't even know himself. He had veered from charm to almost silence within the space of a few hours, and she wondered why. Perhaps she would never know. There she was wrong. She was soon to find out, far sooner than she could imagine.

It was after three in the morning when they went into the lift and up to the flat. Arwenna was tipsy, she knew she was, but there was nothing she could do about it. She stumbled slightly going down the steps into the lounge, and both Garth and Jason took an arm and half carried her to the settee. 'Whee!' she sighed, and hiccuped. 'Oh, do excuse me!' she giggled helplessly, and Jason said to no one in particular:

'I think I'll make some nice strong coffee,' and strode away. Arwenna dropped her bag beside her. It contained nine hundred pounds in twenty-pound notes. She had never even seen that much before, let alone possessed it, but Jason had been adamant. It was hers, the matter was closed. She couldn't think as clearly as she would have liked, but it seemed as if in some way the money was going to help her with something. She didn't have a headache, or any unpleasant sensation connected with drinking. She felt delightfully happy, as if some weighty problem had been resolved, and all was well with the world. It was quite sufficient for her. In the morning, if it ever came, she would try and work out why.

Garth had left her, and Arwenna kicked off her sandals and lay back comfortably on the soft cushions of the settee, closing her eyes. Memories of the evening danced in her head. Their arrival, seeing them in the mirror, the meal, the people, playing roulette, and afterwards cards, and drinking more champagne ... all wonderfully hazy but colourful.

'Okay, take a sip.' Jason offered her a cup, and she took it.

'What is it?'

'Coffee.'

'Oh.' She sipped and pulled a face. 'Ugh, it's strong!'

'Mmm, I know. You're slightly sloshed.'

'So I am.' She laughed. 'And I'm very happy.'

'Lucky girl—to be happy *and* rich. Very nice.'

'But I don't feel as if it's mine—I didn't mean that——'

'Please, no more,' he ordered. 'I won too, you know. Not as much as you—but enough. My dear Arwenna, I was delighted to see you doing so well. I've had a good evening too, and that's yours to do as you wish. Buy some clothes with it—you're going to France next week, aren't you? Well then, buy an outfit to knock 'em dead with.'

'No, I'm not,' she said, and was aware, as she spoke that Garth had reappeared.

'Not going to knock 'em dead?' asked Jason, amused. 'Okay, put it in the bank.'

'No, I didn't mean that.' She put her cup down. 'I mean I'm not going to France.' The words fell into a still, small silence, and she saw Jason glance up towards Garth. And then—something changed. She could feel it, sense the growing sudden tension in the room, and her heartbeats quickened. She had said what was in her mind, almost without thinking about it, her tongue loosened by champagne, and it had been the correct thing to say at the time. Only now, too late, she knew she shouldn't have.

Slowly, very slowly, she looked up at Garth. So did Jason, who stood, as if at a signal from the other man, said: 'Excuse me,' and walked away from them. Then he'd gone, taking his coffee with him, and she knew he wouldn't be back.

'That's news to me,' said Garth. 'May I ask why?'

'No, you may not,' she answered. 'I'm going to bed when I've drunk this,' and she picked up her cup. The next moment it had been taken from her, and she was being pulled to her feet. Startled, she looked into Garth's face, and saw an anger greater than anything she had ever seen before. She wriggled to free herself, but he held her in a steel-like grip and repeated:

'Why?'

'Let me go!'

'When you've told me.'

Her head was clearing with shock and she looked calmly at him. 'I don't want to go with you,' she said. 'That's why.'

'That is not a good enough reason,' he said softly. 'We have an agreement, remember?'

'I've been thinking about our "agreement",' she answered. 'And about a lot of other things—and about you. And I've come to my senses.' She reached out and prised his fingers from her arm, then from the other one. 'I don't want to go anywhere with you. And before you remind me of my aunt, and about James' father, and all the other little bits of blackmail you've tried, I'll tell *you* something. I'm going to pay back every penny of what it's cost for Aunt Daisy to have the operation, and for having those two women running the café. I was going to anyway, I'd already decided that today, but what I won tonight will help. And as for James' father, I've realised—belatedly—that I'm not responsible for other people's lives. I'll see him when I get home, and tell him what you did, and it's up to him to sort something out—not me. You've tried to take over my life, and you nearly succeeded, but that's over now. I'll return the money you gave me, and——'

'You've said enough,' he cut in. 'You'd better get to bed. We'll talk in the morning.' His voice was hard and angry.

'I haven't finished,' she shot back. 'Just because you don't like what I say——'

'No, I don't. But I'm in no mood to argue with a drunken woman.'

'I'm not drunk!'

'I don't know what the hell you are, then.'

She stood in front of him, wishing she were a man. She was trembling with reaction, and anger, and she hated the hard, scornful look on his face, as though she were being stupid. 'Damn you,' she whispered. 'Who the hell do you think *you* are?'

'I know who I am.'

'You're ruthless!'

'Yes, I am. So are you in your own way——'

He got no further. Arwenna struck out at him and he caught her hand and pulled her up to him—the coffee cup was knocked, went flying over her skirt, staining it badly.

'Oh!' she gasped, and looked at it. Then, turning, she ran away from him and into the bedroom. She closed the door and stripped off her skirt and took it into the bathroom to sponge it, then her door crashed open and Garth came in, white-faced.

'Get out!' she snapped. He followed her into the bathroom. She wore a waist slip beneath the skirt, and that too had been caught. She turned to him as she filled the bowl with cold water. 'Will you go?' she demanded.

'No. We'll finish this now—one way or the other.'

'You said I was drunk before——'

'You're not. You're as sober as I am.'

She pushed past him, into the bedroom, and put on her dressing gown. Icily she stared at him. 'I'm going to take off my slip,' she said. 'You've ruined that as well. I hope you're satisfied!'

'If you hadn't landed out at me it wouldn't have happened.'

She ignored that and slipped the underskirt off, carried that into the bathroom and began soaking the affected parts with cold water, gently and carefully, though with an effort to control her temper. When she was satisfied, she rolled both up in her towel, then laid them over the side of the bath.

'There's nothing more to say,' she told him. 'So it's useless you waiting—and don't try any of your strong-arm tactics on me. That won't persuade me to listen to you. I've had enough from you, all I'm going to take——'

'And where will you stay until your aunt is well enough to leave the clinic? Here?' he asked.

'No! I'll go—Steve and Zack will put me up. Don't worry, I'll manage.'

'I'm sure you will,' he answered icily. 'That should be nice for you, sleeping in one large room with—how many—four young men? You'll enjoy that won't you?'

'You can sneer as much as you like. I'll be *safer* there than I am here,' she snapped. 'At least they've never made a pass at me!'

'Don't be so naïve. Probably because they've never had the chance!'

She tried to push past him, to go into the bedroom, incensed, trying not to listen, but he caught her and held her, struggling in his arms. 'You stay here,' he said, voice low and cold.

'No, damn you, I won't!' Her eyes were wide and brilliant, lit with the anger that consumed her. 'In fact, I'll go now. Do you hear that? *Now!*'

Garth shook her hard, as if caught by something beyond his reasoning, and then, with a groan, took her to him, and kissed her.

Sobbing, frightened at his violence, Arwenna struggled to free herself, but it was impossible. She hated him, she hated herself—she hated his kiss—only then suddenly, moments later, she didn't. It was a savage, punishing kiss, intended as such by a man nearly beyond reason, and she fought and struggled to escape his mouth at first, then, as she went lightheaded with the combined effects of alcohol and anger, she found herself, to her horror, responding with a fierceness to match her previous resistance.

It was no use. Her own confused emotions were too much for her to cope with. The kiss changed, deepened, became more intense, and she sensed his growing excitement and responded with her own, helplessly.

'Dear God,' he whispered, after an age, 'you drive me insane,' and he buried his face in her thick tumble of hair, holding her as if he would never let her go.

'You're hurting me,' she said, voice shaking. 'Please——'

'I want to hurt you. Oh God, I want to——' His hands were upon her, and she trembled at his touch, her senses responding in a way she understood only too well, now, to his feverish lovemaking. He was a man almost beyond control, and she whimpered with pain as he suddenly pushed her away and staggered towards the bed, and sat down as if he could no longer stand. Anguished, she saw him go, then followed him, and struck out at his shoulder, sobbing with sudden anger at the rejection.

'Go—get *out*!' she shouted, voice torn, and Garth reached up, put his hands up to shield his face as if he could no longer defend himself from her attack, and Arwenna, knowing it, pushed his hands away and struck him. 'I hate you!'

She stumbled with the force of her own anger, fell against him, and the next moment they were in a tangled heap on the bed, and she was pummelling his chest with her fists, and crying.

He had no strength left, or so it seemed for a few moments, as he neither resisted nor defended himself —then, as though with a supreme effort, he found strength and caught her flailing arms, and said, brokenly : 'I can't fight you.'

'Then go—get out of my life!' she sobbed, the tears coursing down her face, her body against his, legs quivering with the effort to get balance again, but she couldn't, and, weakened by her own efforts at resistance, at struggling against such an overwhelming force as he, she lay back at last, panting and exhausted. Garth leaned over her, looking down at her, and his eyes were very dark, and his face shadowed, with deep lines of pain etched there, a man who had reached the end of his tether.

He groaned and said her name as if it hurt him, then again, then he leaned down his head and rested it against her breast, and closed his eyes. Arwenna could feel that he was trembling. She felt the tremors course through her own body, and she lifted up her arms and held them round him, to still the anguish that communicated itself to her.

'Oh, Garth,' she whispered. 'It's no use—don't you see—we'll destroy ourselves——' She held him closely to her, torn with love and despair for this man she would trust with her life, whom she loved more than life itself, but who would never love her, because he didn't know what love was, and because of that knowledge she had to go, to get out of his life and be safe. She was sure that she brought out the worst in him as well, and that was the terrible thing. She had seen him with others, with his friends, and he was different, charming, well liked. Ruthless, yes, in business certainly—and with her—only with her. There's something wrong with us both, she thought, as she felt him relaxing against her, gradually losing the tension and overwhelming anger that had filled him. Some chemistry that's triggered off whenever we are alone. Something dreadful and beyond the understanding of us both.

Oh, my darling, she thought. If only you knew my feelings for you! Lying there, closely, with him, was sweet torment. To touch, to hold him, to know his kiss and the caress of his hands, was more than she could bear. His body was hard and muscular, relaxed now in the calm after the storm, and perhaps now that the fury had abated she could say what she had to, and he would listen.

'Whatever happens, whatever you decide,' she whispered, 'I can't stay. I know you want me, I know you said we ought to get each other out of our systems, and in a way you're probably right. But it's not my way. I've known you for only a week, and my life is altered. Don't you see? I must be free.'

'I know,' he said, so softly that she barely heard the words. 'I know——' and he groaned and moved slightly away from her, lifting his hand to lay it on her cheek, then closed his eyes. His face was shadowed in the soft light that came from the bathroom; she hadn't switched on the bedroom lamp. She saw his mouth move, as though he tried to speak, but no words came, then he put down his head, and his body was shaking, as though he was weeping.

It was more than she could bear. She cried out something, softly, and cradled his head against her breast, soothing him as a mother soothes a child, then she kissed his cheek, murmuring words she didn't understand herself, seeking only to release him from the intolerable prison of his pain.

Gradually he became still, and the minutes passed with no words spoken, and at last Arwenna knew that he was asleep. She leaned over very carefully and pulled up the coverlet from the floor, his side, and covered them both. Then she too fell asleep, in his arms.

It was already light when she awoke. Garth was fast asleep, and his arms were round her as if he would never let her go, and her lips were touching his hair so that she tasted the faint sweetness of it. They had slept for how long—perhaps four hours. She dared not move to look at the clock, for fear of disturbing him. It was the first time she had slept with him, and undoubtedly the last. Soon she was going to leave him. If he stayed on in Raneley she would see him again, that was unavoidable; it was not a big place, but they would never be alone, she would make sure of that. And once Aunt Daisy was fully recovered, Arwenna might go away again, if life proved impossible—if she still loved him.

He stirred in his sleep, then, as if realising where he was, made a sound in his throat, a questioning sound.

'It's all right,' she said. 'We fell asleep.'

He sat up and rubbed his hair. 'Here? I've been *here*?'

'Yes.' She began to get off the bed, but his hand clamped over her wrist.

'You let me stay?' he asked huskily.

She shivered. It was cool, even with the dressing gown on. 'Your reputation is safe,' she murmured. 'I shan't tell anyone. And if you leave now, Jason won't know.'

Slowly, inexorably, Garth drew her towards him. Then he kissed her. This time she didn't struggle. Her senses were still blurred from sleep; his arms were warm and very strong—and gentle. She put her hand to his heart, and it was quickening, beating strongly and faster than normal. The heady longing turned to fire, and it was no longer cool. She was burning, burning. The skin of his face was rough with stubble, but she scarcely noticed, for she was lost in the heady sweetness of his lips as they searched hers.

All was lost, timeless, beyond logic or reason. She knew nothing any more save the bliss of being with him that carried her away from the world she knew into another place, another time . . .

Arwenna looked back once as she went out of the door, and made a small kiss with her mouth. Goodbye, she thought, goodbye. She could not stay. She could not face him. Even though she loved him, nothing had been resolved between them.

She gathered up her clothes and crept out, leaving Garth sleeping inside her bed. She unlocked the door with her key, put the key on the table where he would find it, and went towards the lift. It was eight o'clock on Sunday morning, and when she was outside she was going to telephone Steve and ask him if he would collect her.

She took the lift to the basement and walked out into the street, looking for a telephone box. There had been no time or desire to pack. She had what she stood up in, and her toothbrush, and handbag. The streets were quiet, no one about, and the telephone rang for a while before Steve himself answered it, sounding half asleep, and not a little annoyed.

'Steve? It's Arwenna.'

'Arwenna?' He was instantly alert. 'What is it? This sounds like a pay phone. Where are you?'

'Can you come and meet me?' she begged. 'I've left Garth's flat—I need somewhere to stay.'

'I'm on my way. Where's the phone booth?'

'Just round the corner from the flats. I'm sorry to call you, but I've nowhere to go——'

'Stay *right* there. Are you okay?'

'Yes, I'm all right.'

'Thank God! I don't want to know why you need me—but you do, and that's enough. Hang up, love, and let me get started.'

'All right. I'll be here. 'Bye.'

She hung up and remained in the booth. Fifteen minutes later a bright orange Mini screeched to a halt outside the kiosk, and half an hour after that she was sitting in the small kitchen of the flat drinking hot tea and eating burnt toast, and recovering slowly.

They spoke in whispers. Snores issued from the living room, which was also a bedroom for four, and three sleeping men didn't even know they had a female visitor.

Steve had closed the door, sat her down by the window and put the kettle on. 'You'd better tell me what happened,' he said.

She shook her head. 'Not yet. I'm not sure myself.' Which was a lie, but if she told him the truth he might go round to Garth's apartment and start tearing the place apart. She didn't want any trouble like that. She had already had enough to last a few lifetimes, in less than a week.

'I just decided I couldn't stay any longer. We—we don't get on,' she sighed. 'There's a complete clash of personalities. I just ran out—cowardly, I know, but it seemed the only way. I'm sorry to drag you out of bed, but I had nowhere else to——'

'Listen—hey, love, it's *me*, Steve, remember? Considering I'd quite happily climb the highest mountain, crawl over broken glass, etcetera, etcetera—do you think I mind coming out at eight on a Sunday morning to save you? You've got to be kidding!'

She laughed, near to tears, and buried her head against his chest as he put his arms round her and hugged her. 'Oh, I don't deserve you,' she said.

'Well, you've got me—for as long as you want me. You've not fallen for him, have you?' He drew away and looked suspiciously at her.

'I'm afraid I have.'

'Hell's bells! I can hardly go and duff him up now, can I?' She shook her head, biting her lip. 'Does he know where you are?'

'No. When I left, he was still asleep.'

'Is he likely to phone—see if you're here?'

'I don't know.'

'If he does, do I say yes or no?'

'Tell him. It's better—he might worry. Yes, it's better.'

'Okay. Now, I don't know exactly where you're going to sleep tonight, but we've got a day to fix something up. When does your aunt come out of the clinic?'

'I'll find out tomorrow. I didn't think about the finer points of everything—Oh, Steve, I'm so tired!' She had had very little sleep for ages, and it was telling at last.

He nodded. 'You look it. Look, get into my bed and I'll crawl on to the settee for a while, then when they wake me up, I'll—ahem—warn them you're here.'

'You're an angel!' she smiled mistily.

'I know,' he grinned. 'I might as well go down and collect the Sunday papers and do a crossword or something. Come on, bed.'

Five minutes later Arwenna was fast asleep in his bed.

When she woke up the room was empty, and fairly tidy, and she was alone.

She sat up and looked round her, puzzled. A large piece of paper was pinned on the settee, and she went over, yawning, to read it. 'Dear A,' it said, 'We've all adjourned to the pub to let you get your beauty sleep. If you want to come down it's the Oddfellows Arms at the end of the road on left. We've fixed up a bed for tonight. I had to restrain Zack from ravishing you as you slept. Back at two, Steve.'

She looked at her watch. One-thirty. They must have woken and crept out. She felt better, but not much. She washed in the kitchen and then set out to do the stack of unwashed dishes piled precariously on the draining board. When they were done she found a carpet sweeper and duster and began to work in the living room, dusting an incredibly untidy mantelpiece, when the door opened and she turned to see Garth walking in.

She froze, panicked, and sent a small ashtray flying into the hearth. For a moment it seemed as if her heart stopped beating. He looked across the room at her, then walked towards her.

'All right,' he said. 'I don't know what you want, but you can have it.' His words didn't make sense. Arwenna stood there motionless, duster still clutched in one hand, and gazed at him.

'Why—are you here?' she asked at last.

'Why do you think?' He looked haggard and almost ill, but he managed a faint smile. 'It's where I knew you'd be.'

'You must know why I left,' she said faintly. 'After —what happened—it's impossible——'

'I know. That's what I told myself when I discovered you'd gone. I know what we do to each other, and you're quite right—only it hit me so hard that it was like a physical ache inside me. I didn't mean it to happen like this, Arwenna, but, God help me, life suddenly had no meaning any more. I love you. I don't think I can live without you. If you don't come back, I'll have a damned good try—but it won't be worth much.' He took hold of her hands, and she felt the fine tremor in his. 'I couldn't even drive my car here, I had to get Jason to bring me. He's outside. I know all you accused me of—and you were right. I was taking over —because I was frightened of being taken over. I've never said this to anyone before—but I need you. For God's sake don't send me away.' His voice broke, became husky. 'Say something, even if it's only Go to hell!'

She shook her head. 'I don't want to say that. Don't you know why I left? Can't you guess?'

'I can guess. You told me last night why.'

'No, not only that. I found out—on Euston Station

to be precise, at about seven in the morning, when you kissed me because that policeman was watching—that I'd done something very stupid. I discovered that I'd fallen rather badly for you.' She looked slowly at the hands that held hers, then back to his face. His beloved, wonderful, gentle face. 'But I never dreamed I'd hear you say you loved me.'

'We've only known each other a week. It's madness, I know that. I don't do mad, stupid things. I'm hard and realistic, and I know that love's an illusion—I know all this, Arwenna, with the practical side of me, and yet,' he lifted one hand to touch her cheek, to smooth the soft skin, 'and yet, when I see you, my heart lifts, when I touch you, like this, it's so special and wonderful, that I know there's no illusion. I love you for what you are, for what you have become, in a short time, a special person to me, someone I want to love and cherish for as long as I live.'

He took her in his arms then, enfolded her tightly, and held her to him. 'It's no good us fighting it any more. And I was fighting it—and you—because I tried to deny that I could ever need anyone. I've lost that fight—I knew I'd lost it when I found you gone.'

Arwenna smiled, but it was one of delicious anticipation. 'Oh, Garth, I wanted you so much, and I tried to deny that too. I've never wanted any man before.'

'Will you go to France with me—as my wife?' he asked. 'Will you marry me and come with me wherever I go—and wherever you want to go, and stay with me for ever and ever?'

'You know I will.'

He gave a deep sigh. 'There'll be no more quarrels. I love you too much to ever hurt you. We're both strong personalities, and we may not always agree, but we'll work it out together, one way or another.' He kissed her very gently. 'Where are your two friends?'

'At the pub. I was just tidying up——'

'So I see,' he said gravely. 'We'd better wait for them, hadn't we? They both love you—and I know why now. Do you think they'll be heartbroken?'

She shook her head, smiling. 'I don't think so, somehow. They're special friends—always will be.'

'Then I'll have to look after you, or else I can see——'

As Garth said the words, the door opened, and Steve and Zack came in. They were carrying several cans of beer.

'Oh,' said Steve.

'Oh, no!' sighed Zack. They looked from Arwenna to Garth, and back again.

Garth gently released her. 'I'm sorry,' he said, 'but I'm afraid you've just lost your new flatmate.'

Steve looked at Zack, who gave a resigned shrug. 'We're going to be married,' said Garth.

Zack crossed over to Arwenna. 'Do you love him?' he asked.

She nodded. 'Yes.'

'Aw, hell!' He glared at Garth, then stuck his hand out. Solemnly they shook hands. 'Look after her, or I'll kill you,' Zack said pleasantly.

'I know—and I will. That's a promise. I don't suppose it's any use asking you to the wedding?'

Zack shrugged. 'You could try. Where's the reception? I've never been to the Ritz, actually.'

'Why not? We'll let you know the time and date. Thanks for looking after her.' He took Arwenna's hand, and she gently disengaged herself and went to kiss both Steve and Zack.

'Goodbye. Thanks for everything. I'll be in touch.' Her eyes were shining. Then she and Garth walked out, and down to the car where Jason waited.

CHAPTER TWELVE

BUT there was more. When they were both in his apartment, and Jason had vanished discreetly—sensing perhaps that he was no longer needed, Garth told her the final truth.

They sat comfortably side by side on the settee near the window; it was Sunday afternoon, sunny outside, a perfect day. 'You know, Jason didn't come here by chance,' he said. 'He told me after you'd gone out. He'd come to see you.'

'Me? But he didn't even know——'

'Ah, but he did. He'd heard via the grapevine about the little incident with Marcia, and also had a word with Lucy, whom he knows—her lover is an old chum of his—and Lucy had found you a fascinating person, and told him that she suspected not only that you might take Marcia's place, but that she could see me falling head over heels.'

Arwenna began to laugh, softly, eyes shining. 'Dear Lucy,' she murmured.

'Quite. All this intrigued Jason sufficiently to "drop in" by chance—and get to know you.' He hugged her. 'And he agreed. He thinks you're quite special.'

'I like him too.'

'As long as that's all,' he growled, and kissed her.

'Of course,' she agreed. 'How could I ever look at another man? I've got you. Oh, Garth, I do love you, truly.'

He stroked her hand thoughtfully. 'There's more,' he said softly.

'More? About Jason—why?'

'No, about me.'

She was intrigued. There was something in his voice ...

'Go on,' she said, her heart thudding.

'Four months ago, when I went back to Raneley for the first time in fifteen years—I was in the estate agent's car, and it had stopped at the lights—you crossed the road in front of us. I saw you, and something odd happened to me. I can't explain what it was because nothing like it had ever happened before—but I had to know who you were. I asked the agent, very casually, and he told me.'

'Old Mr Brown? I've known him for years.' She smiled.

'So he said. As he drove me to Raneley Hall he told me all about you—and I knew then that I was going to get to know you, one way or another. He also told me that you were engaged to James Rhodes. It was enough. My dearest love, you didn't have a chance after that day—although you didn't know it.'

'You angled it so that you could get to know the Colonel, didn't you?'

'Mmm.'

'You crafty devil!'

'You could say that.' Garth laughed and pulled her to him. 'How does it feel, knowing you'll never get away from me again?'

She turned her face towards his, put her hands up to his face, and touched his cheeks gently. 'Let me show you,' she said, and kissed him.

One book by a favorite author
is a treasure!

Three books
by a
favorite author
is a

Harlequin
Omnibus

Three great love stories
in one giant-sized volume –
A book to cherish!

◆ Harlequin
Omnibus

The great
three-in-one
way to collect
love stories by your
favorite authors!

Stories that share
the joy, wonder and
happiness of being
in love.

A new
Harlequin Omnibus
every month!

Wherever paperback books are sold.

FREE!
Romance Treasury

**A beautifully bound,
value-packed,
three-in-one
volume of romance!**

FREE!

A hardcover Romance Treasury volume containing 3 treasured works of romance by 3 outstanding Harlequin authors...

...as your introduction to Harlequin's Romance Treasury subscription plan!

...almost 600 pages of exciting romance reading every month at the low cost of $5.97 a volume!

A wonderful way to collect many of Harlequin's most beautiful love stories, all originally published in the late '60s and early '70s. Each value-packed volume, bound in a distinctive gold-embossed leatherette case and wrapped in a colorfully illustrated dust jacket, contains...
- 3 full-length novels by 3 world-famous authors of romance fiction
- a unique illustration for every novel
- the elegant touch of a delicate bound-in ribbon bookmark... and much, much more!

Romance Treasury

...for a library of romance you'll treasure forever!

Complete and mail today the FREE gift certificate and subscription reservation on the following page.

Romance Treasury

An exciting opportunity to collect treasured works of romance! Almost 600 pages of exciting romance reading in each beautifully bound hardcover volume!

You may cancel your subscription whenever you wish! You don't have to buy any minimum number of volumes. Whenever you decide to stop your subscription just drop us a line and we'll cancel all further shipments.

FREE GIFT!
Certificate and Subscription Reservation

Mail this coupon today to
Harlequin Reader Service

In the U.S.A.	In Canada
1440 South Priest Drive	649 Ontario Street
Tempe, AZ 85281	Stratford, Ontario N5A 6W2

Please send me my FREE Romance Treasury volume. Also, reserve a subscription to the new Romance Treasury published every month. Each month I will receive a Romance Treasury volume at the low price of $5.97 plus 75¢ for postage and handling (total—$6.72). There are no hidden charges. I am free to cancel at any time, but if I do, my FREE Romance Treasury volume is mine to keep, without any obligation.

NAME _____

(Please Print)

ADDRESS _____

CITY _____

STATE/PROV. _____

ZIP/POSTAL CODE _____

Offer expires January 31, 1982
Offer not valid to present subscribers.

B2418